THE GREAT CHOCOLATE SCAM

Sally Berneathy

Books by Sally Berneathy

Death by Chocolate
(book 1 in the Death by Chocolate series)

Murder, Lies and Chocolate
(book 2 in the Death by Chocolate series)

The Great Chocolate Scam
(book 3 in the Death by Chocolate series)

Chocolate Mousse Attack
(book 4 in the Death by Chocolate series)

Fatal Chocolate Obsession
(book 5 in the Death by Chocolate series)

Deadly Chocolate Addiction
(book 6 in the Death by Chocolate series)

Guns, Wives and Chocolate
(book 7 in the Death by Chocolate series)

Spies, Lies and Chocolate Pies
(book 8 in the Death by Chocolate series)

The Ex Who Wouldn't Die
(book 1 in Charley's Ghost series)

The Ex Who Glowed in the Dark
(book 2 in Charley's Ghost series)

The Ex Who Conned a Psychic
(book 3 in Charley's Ghost series)

The Ex Who Saw a Ghost
(book 4 in Charley's Ghost series)

The Ex Who Hid a Deadly Past
(book 5 in Charley's Ghost series)

Chapter One

Three fifteen on a hot Monday afternoon in July. I sat in the client chair in my lawyer's office, tapping my foot and fidgeting. Rick was fifteen minutes late for our appointment to sign the divorce papers.

Based on the last couple of years of his flip-flopping between *I want a divorce* and *I want you back*, I suppose I shouldn't have been surprised. But this time he'd seemed desperate to get it done as soon as possible. In fact, he was disappointed we had to wait a week for our attorneys to find a mutually available time to get together.

I figured he was in love again. He hadn't said so, but that was usually the reason he was ready to sign off on the divorce. Rick fell in love regularly. He fell out just as quickly, but that would soon no longer be my problem.

I was looking forward to being a free woman with no more ties to Rickhead, to owning one hundred percent of my little restaurant, Death by Chocolate located in Pleasant Grove, a suburb of Kansas City, and to dating Detective Adam Trent officially. Soon Rick couldn't show up at my front door with protestations of eternal love or plans for some barely-legal scheme that somehow involved me. Well, he could still show up and try to involve me, but he wouldn't be able to use the lever of signing the divorce papers to get me to aid and abet him.

I had even bought a new outfit to wear to my lawyer's office for the big event, a dark purple raw silk pantsuit with a turquoise and lavender scarf. Very elegant and stylish. My friend, Paula, went with me to pick it out. When clothing goes beyond blue jeans and T-shirts, I'm lost.

So I sat there in the office of Jason Beckwirth of Hampton, Grier, Morris and Beckwirth, looking elegant and stylish and irritated, waiting for my former knight in tarnished armor to show up and make me the happiest woman in the world by agreeing to unmarry me.

Why wasn't I waiting at my father's law firm? Because divorce is beneath them. They're corporate lawyers handling real estate deals, tax law, estate planning, that sort of *respectable* law. Besides that, he and Mom blamed me for the failure of a marriage they'd tried to prevent. After trashing him for years, suddenly when I announced I was divorcing Rick, he became their favorite son-in-law. I'm an only child, so that was really no great feat.

Jason looked up from the papers he was studying and smiled. He has a deceptively genial expression, looks like the boy next door, but he turns into the cut-throat lawyer next door in the courtroom. "Relax," he said. "They'll be here any minute. You know Rick will be late to his own funeral."

I crossed my legs and changed to swinging instead of tapping. "This waiting makes me nervous. I don't trust him."

Jason nodded. "With good reason. But when I talked to his lawyer last week, he said Rick was adamant about going through with this. You sure I can't get you a cup of coffee?"

"No, but a Coke would be good." I'd only had one so far that day. Our breakfast and lunch crowds at the restaurant were hectic and hungry, so Paula and I had been too busy to do much eating or drinking ourselves. My stomach rumbled and reminded me about the eating part.

Jason called his assistant, and she brought me a glass of Coke with ice. I preferred my Coke straight, no melting ice to dilute it, but at that moment, I would have settled for a Pepsi.

I finished the soft drink, swung my right leg then my left, tapped my feet, drummed my fingers and waited.

No Rick.

The beige phone on Jason's desk jangled—in a dignified manner, of course. Jason glanced at the display. "It's Bert," he said and lifted the receiver.

Bert Hanson, Rick's lawyer.

I inhaled sharply. I tried to tell myself he was probably calling to say they were stuck in traffic, but my heart sank down to the tip of my little toe. I had a horrible feeling Rick was jacking me around again. His lawyer was calling to say he'd cancelled.

I watched Jason's face, listened to every word he said, strained to hear the other side of the conversation. I couldn't, of course. My neighbor Fred probably could have if he'd been there. I'm pretty sure Fred has super powers. Not that I've seen him flying or anything like that.

Yet.

Jason didn't say much. "I see." He looked at me and shook his head. That was a bad sign. "Okay. Well, thanks for letting me know."

He cradled the receiver, then lifted his gaze and folded his hands on his desk. "Lindsay—"

"He's not coming, is he?"

Jason sighed and shook his head. "It doesn't look like it. He didn't show up at Bert's office, and Bert hasn't been able to reach him by phone."

"Damn it!" I slammed my hand on the arm of the chair, shot up and spun around. I needed to go outside, run, hit something, eat huge quantities of chocolate. I needed to vent the anger that flared up inside me. This time I'd dared to hope. This time I really thought it was going to happen. This time the disappointment was even worse than usual.

I thought about the night on the town Trent and I had planned in celebration. The Divorcement Party I'd scheduled for Saturday night. None of it was going to happen. Rick was still causing problems, still controlling my life.

I stomped to one side of the room then back to the other, cursing with vehemence and sincerity. "Damn it, damn it, damn it! I knew it! That sorry, worthless, no-good—"

My cell phone began to play George Strait's *Blue Clear Sky*, Trent's ringtone.

"I'm sorry." I strode over to my purse and pulled out the phone to send the call to voicemail, but decided maybe I should answer and tell Trent I'd return his call in a couple of minutes. There was no reason for me to stay in Jason's office any longer. We weren't going to do business that day.

"Hi, Trent. Can I call you right back?"

"No."

"No?"

"I need to talk to you right now. I wanted you to hear this from me before you see it on television."

On television? No good news ever got reported on television. "Okay, fine, hang on and let me say good-bye to Jason. I'm just leaving my attorney's office. Rick was a no show."

"I know."

"You do?" Fred was the one who always knew things. Apparently Trent had just developed psychic abilities too.

"There's been an accident."

My insides went cold at that sentence, and I sank back down into my chair. The cops on TV said those words when they came to tell a family about a death. Images of the people I cared about most whirled through my mind. My parents, Fred, Paula, Zach, Henry... "What kind of accident? Who?"

He paused for what seemed like an hour but was probably closer to a second. "It's Rick. There was an explosion. His car was blown up in his driveway."

I frowned, relieved and puzzled. That explained why he hadn't shown up for our meeting. He'd have trouble driving if his car exploded. "An accident? Rick's a terrible mechanic, but blowing up his own car seems like quite a feat even for him."

"He didn't blow it up. Somebody else did. Lindsay, you need to come down to the station."

"Why? Are you craving my chocolate chip cookies?" I was grasping at straws. I could tell from the somber tone of his voice that he wasn't trying to wheedle cookies.

"We need to ask you some questions." He paused again, and I could hear him draw in a deep breath. "Rick was in the car when it blew up. Lindsay, Rick's dead."

Chapter Two

I left Jason's office in a daze.

Rick was dead.

A man I'd once loved, been married to, planned a life with, was gone forever from this earth. I'd never again see those blue eyes enhanced by colored contacts, that arrogant smile, that carefully streaked blond hair.

A part of me was sad, but I have to admit that a tiny part of me was just a little bit relieved. Rick had driven me crazy with his cheating while we were married, then after we separated he'd switched to just driving me crazy in general. Even though the separation was his idea...out with the old (Lindsay), in with the new (Muffy)...as soon as he and Muffy broke up, he decided he wanted me back. I, on the other hand, decided that one burst of insanity—marrying him in the first place—was enough for one lifetime and told him I wasn't coming back.

He didn't get to be top salesman for Rheims Commercial Real Estate by accepting *no* for an answer, and he had no intention of accepting *no* from me. I became a challenge, that big sale he was having trouble closing.

Then he met Becky and backed off for a while until Becky became history. After that came Carolyn, Vanessa, Lisa and probably a few more I didn't know about. The last couple of years had been stressful, frustrating and maddening. This sudden and very final resolution seemed somehow too abrupt and a little anticlimactic. After all the hassle, it just couldn't be this easy.

I drove to the police station, and Trent met me at the front desk. He was a welcome sight in his rumpled jacket and slacks. He has great eyes, brown with hints of green. The happier he is, the more green shows in his eyes. That day his eyes were brown like the bark on a tree in winter, and his expression was grim.

He came over to me, wrapped me in his arms and hugged me in front of God, the dispatcher and everybody. Since my divorce wasn't final, we had never indulged in public displays of affection. This public hug made the new circumstances suddenly real. My divorce was final.

"I'm sorry, Lindsay," Trent murmured in my ear.

As soon as he released me, his partner, Gerald Lawson, took his place, embracing me gently. My nickname for Gerald is Granite Man. He's tall and thin with structured gray hair and a face that never shows emotion. From the first time I met him, I've had a goal to break him down, to make him show some kind of emotion, maybe even toss caution to the wind and laugh without restraint. Seems I cracked the granite that day, but not the way I intended. When he pulled back, his expression was marked with sadness and sympathy.

I felt a little guilty, accepting all that compassion under false pretenses. Sure, I was upset that Rick was dead, but in a detached sort of way, the same way I'd feel upset over the death of a stranger. That's what he had become. An annoying stranger.

The boys led me into an interrogation room with a scarred wooden table, uncomfortable wooden chairs and a one-way mirror. Suddenly I felt like a criminal rather than the object of sympathy. Surely they didn't think...

"We're sorry for your loss." Lawson sat across from me. He had resumed his Granite Man face.

"My loss?"

"Your deceased husband."

I flinched and stole a glance at Trent who sat next to Lawson. We'd been sort of dating for several months, waiting for my divorce to be final before putting a name to our relationship, and I wondered how he felt about his partner's reference to my *husband*. However, at that moment Trent, whom Fred referred to as Mr. Stone Face because of the stern way his chiseled features looked when he was playing cop, wasn't showing much more expression than Granite Man.

"My *ex* husband," I said.

"Your divorce wasn't final."

"I think it is now. I think this is about as final as it's going to get."

Lawson nodded and looked down at the papers lying on the table in front of him before once again lifting his steely gaze. "Where were you at three o'clock this afternoon?"

I half rose out of my chair. "Where was I? You think I blew him up? You seriously think I would go to all the trouble to blow him up when I was just about to get what I wanted from him?"

"No!" Trent reached a hand across the table toward me. I refused to meet him halfway and take his hand, but I did sit back down.

"We have to ask," Lawson said.

"I was sitting in my lawyer's office, waiting for Rick to arrive and sign the divorce papers." I gave them Jason's name and phone number. "You can check with him, and I'll give you a copy of his bill for all that wasted time." I glared at both of them in turn. See if I ever made them chocolate chip cookies again.

"So Rick was on his way to your lawyer's office?"

"He was going to his lawyer's office first, then they would come to Jason's office together. He never made it to his lawyer's." I studied the two of them, so sympathetic and caring one minute, so official the next. "If one of you could tell me exactly what happened, I might be able to answer your questions a little better."

Trent looked at me, holding my gaze as if he could support me by the power of his eyes. "The explosion occurred a few minutes after three o'clock in Rick's driveway. Nobody saw it happen, so we're not sure if he had just backed out of the garage or if the car had been sitting there for a while."

"He never left his car sitting in the driveway. He thought that looked tacky, not befitting his status in the neighborhood."

Trent nodded. "The neighbors heard a loud explosion, and parts from the car flew all around the cul-de-sac."

I swallowed and straightened, trying to absorb the image of Rick's green SUV flying around the neighborhood along with pieces of Rick—a blue contact lens in Mrs. Hawkins' driveway, a perfectly creased trouser leg hanging on the street sign. "Do I need to..." I cleared my throat. "Do I need to identify the body?" My voice dropped lower with each word, ending in a whisper.

Trent and Lawson exchanged glances. "No," Lawson said in his matter-of-fact tone. "The body was also blown into a large number of pieces. No one piece is readily identifiable."

I thought I might be sick.

"You're still his wife," Lawson said. "That makes you his next of kin."

I was certain I was going to be sick.

"Do you have the names of other family members?" he continued.

I shook my head and wrapped my arms around myself.

"Did he have other family members?"

"I don't know. I don't think so, but I don't really know. I never met his family. In the beginning, he told me they were on vacation in the Bahamas and couldn't make the wedding. Once he said they lived in New York, then he said they lived abroad. Next his dad was a member of the CIA, and the whole family was on a secret assignment so I couldn't meet them. The next time I asked about his family, he said they were all dead, victims of a terrorist plot, and he'd grown up in orphanages and foster homes. By that time, I'd figured out that pretty much everything Rick said was a lie, so I have no idea if he ever had a family. For all I know, he was actually an alien, stranded here when the mother ship left without him. That would explain a lot."

Lawson nodded. "As next of kin, we will release the victim's remains to you when we conclude our examination of the crime scene."

I turned to Trent. "What did he just say? Am I going to get a box in the mail with two hairs, one toenail and whatever's left of Rick's pancreas?"

Trent flinched. "Not in the mail, but, yeah, that's basically what he said."

"Can't I waive that right? Let you keep whatever you find?"

Trent rose and came around the table to stand beside me. "We'll talk about all that later. How about I drive you home right now? We'll pick up a pizza on the way."

I rose, surprised to find my legs a little shaky. That image of *the victim's remains* didn't set well. "I'm really not hungry right now and I've got my car, but if you want to follow behind and give me a police escort, I'm good with that."

Trent slid an arm around my waist. "I can do that."

I wasn't about to let him know how glad I was for the support. I looked up at him and tried for a smile. "Flashing lights and siren, and I can speed without getting a ticket?"

"No."

I shrugged. "Never hurts to ask."

Chapter Three

I could hear my landline phone ringing as soon as I walked onto my front porch. I opened the door and my cat, King Henry, trotted up, meowing as if in protest at the noise of the phone. Sometimes that cat seems a little psychic, and my first thought was that he was protesting because Rick was on the other end of the phone connection. He never did like Rick. However, my second thought was how unlikely that was. Successful scam artist he was, but even Rick couldn't call from the Great Beyond.

I crossed the living room, leaving the door open for Trent who should be arriving soon with that pizza, and grabbed the receiver. "Hello?"

"I just saw the news, sweetheart. Are you all right?"

My mother. Not Rick, but someone almost as annoying. Verification of Henry's psychic abilities after all.

"I'm fine, Mother. How are you?"

"I am absolutely devastated, and I know you are too."

"Really, I'm not."

"Your father and I have decided you need to come home for a few days, just until this all gets settled. Phoebe's cleaning your old room right now, and she's going to make baked chicken for dinner. I know you don't eat right, all that Coke and chocolate. You need a good meal."

"Thank you, Mother, but I'm just fine where I am."

"You don't have to be so brave, Lindsay. I know you and Rick were having your problems, but he was still your husband."

Leave it to Mom to bring up something I didn't want to hear. "Only through a legal technicality. Don't worry about me, really. I've got Paula next door, Fred on the other side, and Trent's on his way here with a pizza."

"Oh. Trent." I could almost see the icicles forming along the phone line from Mother's house to mine. "Lindsay, I don't know what people are going to think, your spending time with another man when your husband just died."

"And I'm supposed to care what people think...why?"

Henry wound himself around my legs, still complaining. I'd made the phone stop ringing, so I suspected it was now food he wanted. Maybe it had been food all along. Hunger, psychic abilities...it's hard to tell the difference sometimes, especially in cats.

My mother released a long sigh. "Lindsay, I wish you wouldn't be like that. You know how your father and I worry about you."

"Gotta go, Mom. Trent's here with the pizza." He wasn't. Yes, I lied to my mother. It fell under the justifiable umbrella of *lying for a good cause*, in this case to get my mother off the phone before I lost my sanity or Henry starved.

"Lindsay, we have to plan the funeral!"

The funeral? And I'd thought our conversation couldn't get any worse. "Bye, Mom!" I put the receiver down before she could say anything else, though she'd already said enough to send me running for chocolate. "Come on, Henry," I said. "Let's get some stinky food for you and a nice brownie for me."

We went into the kitchen where I poured a large quantity of dry nuggets into Henry's German shepherd sized bowl. He dove in, eating as if he hadn't already consumed a bowl full of the same food that morning. Henry is a large cat, can't even get his head in a regular kitty-sized bowl, and he has an appetite proportionate to his size.

I took a brownie from the freezer and nuked it for twenty seconds then gobbled it as greedily as Henry was scarfing down his food. After waiting in my lawyer's office for Rick to appear, discovering Rick was dead, being grilled about Rick's death, then talking to my mother, I desperately needed a chocolate fix.

The brownie was small, and I was considering some frozen chocolate chip cookie dough when I heard my neighbor, Fred, calling my name from the living room.

"In here!" I took out the container of dough and turned on the oven. Since I had company, I'd be gracious and bake the dough. Fred loves my chocolate chip cookies. Well, who doesn't?

"Anlinny!" A small tornado burst into my kitchen and flung his arms around my legs. I grabbed the edge of the stove to keep from falling. I'll be glad when Zach's a little taller so he can hug me at a more stable height.

He looked up at me, the expression on his angelic face sad, his bright blue eyes intense as only a three-year-old's eyes can be. "Mama says Uncle Rick's gone and you're sad and we have to be nice to you. Can I have cookies?"

"Zachary!" Paula exclaimed. She and Fred both stood in the doorway. My troops had arrived.

Paula moved forward and pulled Zach from his determined embrace. "Being nice to Aunt Lindsay doesn't include knocking her to the floor or asking for cookies!"

"Sure it does." I leaned over and kissed the top of his blond head. "I was just getting ready to make some cookies for Zach, and maybe he'll share with the rest of us."

Zach nodded vigorously. "Okay." He's a generous boy.

Paula released her son who plopped down on the floor and began to annoy Henry. Henry ignored him and continued cleaning out his bowl.

"I'm so sorry," Paula said, coming over to hug me. She's a tiny little thing, blond and delicate, and one of the strongest people I know. "I'm here, whatever you need."

She stood back and Fred came over to offer his hug. I'm tall but he's taller, so much so that he had to lean down for the embrace. "I've got hot dogs, potato salad, and three different flavors of Haagen-Dazs Ice Cream."

Fred's a gourmet cook who often turns up his nose at the stuff I eat, so I was a little surprised that he was offering me hot dogs and potato salad. Then he leaned closer and whispered in my ear, "Independence Day foods. But you really should pretend to be a little upset about Rick's death."

I burst into laughter. I could always count on Fred to put things in their proper perspective.

The front door slammed. "Lindsay?" Trent had arrived with the pizza. We were going to have plenty of food. There's nothing like death to bring out the food from friends and family.

⁂

Fred brought over his contributions to the meal, and we stuffed ourselves. The thought crossed my mind that I should feel a little guilty, enjoying myself with friends and good food when Rick could no longer delight in either of those pleasures. It crossed my mind then darted into oblivion, and I had another helping of Haagen-Dazs Chocolate Peanut Butter Ice Cream.

By nine o'clock Zach and Henry were lying on the floor together, snoozing.

Paula bent down and gathered up her sleeping son. He snuggled into her arms, and she moved toward the front door then stopped. "Do you want to close Death by Chocolate tomorrow?" she asked.

"Close? No. Why would we?" The only time we'd had to close our restaurant was when a crazy woman tried to burn the place down and we had to have repairs made.

"Death in the family."

17

"Oh, that." My mother was probably going to be mortified at my breach of the social mores, but I shook my head firmly. "He's not family. I'll see you in the morning around four."

Only a few months ago a man had been killed outside the restaurant, and I'd created a dessert I called Murdered Man's Brownies which had been a huge success. Maybe I could come up with something in Rick's memory…Rick's Pieces, a chocolate pudding cake with whipped cream containing pieces of chocolate and toffee, or perhaps Rickhead-free Brownies, no gluten, no nuts.

Nah, that was too tacky even for me.

Probably.

We all walked out on my front porch into the warm summer night and Trent, Fred, Henry, and I watched Paula and Zach cross the yard to her house. I was so lucky to have her as a friend.

When she was safely inside with the door closed behind her, Fred moved off the porch. "Call me if you need me no matter what time it is, but only if you really need me. Otherwise, I won't answer."

I'm never quite sure when he's joking.

He strolled toward his house, his lanky frame moving along casually and confidently, his white hair gleaming in the moonlight. I was lucky to have him for a friend too.

Trent wrapped an arm around my waist. Another person I was lucky to have. Interesting how a death can make us appreciate the ones we have left.

I turned to Trent, wrapped my arms around him and kissed him, standing on my porch in full view of anybody who happened to be looking. I was no longer legally married. It didn't matter who saw us together.

When I finally pulled away, we both looked around apprehensively. I halfway expected Rick to burst from behind the nearest bush, charge onto the porch and begin berating me. But that wasn't going to happen ever again, I reminded myself.

"Let's go inside," I suggested, trying to make my voice seductive. "I think I'm as divorced as I'm ever going to be."

He grinned. "Soon," he promised. "But not tonight. You like to act tough and you want everybody to think Rick's death doesn't bother you, but I know it does." He lifted my fingers and brushed them lightly with his lips. "We'll have plenty of time when you're ready."

"I'm ready now," I protested.

"No, you're not."

"Yes, I am."

He kissed me again. Just my opinion, but that was certainly no way to convince me I wasn't ready for him to spend the night with me. "Good night," he said and walked toward his car parked in the street in front of my house.

I waved as he drove away then went back inside. Henry nudged me sleepily as he passed on his way to the stairs that led to our bedroom. I sighed and started to follow him, then paused at the window that looked out onto the street. I couldn't restrain myself from taking one more peek just to be one hundred percent certain Rick wasn't out there spying on me, leaning down from a cloud or pushing up from beneath the sod. Crazy, I know. But he'd done it so many times for so long, I would probably be paranoid the rest of my life.

Of course I saw no sign of him.

But a car parked a couple of houses away started up and moved slowly down the street with no lights on. I held my breath, half expecting to see Rick's SUV. Of course not. That lay in pieces in the police lab. This car was a dark sedan. Just somebody who forgot to turn on his lights. Nothing I should be concerned about.

But the car slowed almost to a stop in front of my house.

I peered closely but couldn't see anything through the tinted windows.

Could the driver see me any more clearly than I could see him?

Suddenly he sped away, turning on his lights when he reached the end of the block.

I was being paranoid.

I checked my door to be sure it was locked and went upstairs to sleep with my cat since my boyfriend had gone home.

Chapter Four

It was almost two o'clock and the lunch crowd was winding down when Bryan Kollar walked in the front door.

Paula was in the back beginning the cleanup, and I was behind the counter at the cash register so I had the experience of his entrance all to myself. The man was even more gorgeous than he looked in the TV ads for his chain of gyms, Body by Bryan. Over six feet tall, black wavy hair, eyes so blue they were almost turquoise, and every muscle in that fabulous body outlined by his tight T-shirt. The room suddenly got ten degrees hotter.

It was only a few minutes before closing time and normally I'd have told anybody who came in that we were closed. But Bryan Kollar wasn't just anybody.

"Can I help you?" I asked, my mouth stretching into a huge smile. Couldn't help myself. How can anyone not smile when viewing something that pleasing to the eyes?

He returned my smile, ramping up the wattage as he approached the counter where I stood. Add another ten degrees to the room temperature.

"I'm looking for Lindsay Kramer."

My smile slipped a little. Only friends of Rick ever called me Lindsay Kramer. I'd kept my birth name of Powell when I married him.

"I'm Lindsay Powell," I said. "I was married to Richard Kramer."

His expression turned sad. "I'm so sorry for your loss."

I shrugged. "Thanks. What can I do for you?" It suddenly occurred to me that I, as Rick's only surviving relative, could be liable for his debts. Had Rick borrowed money from this rich, famous man or scammed him out of money? But surely this man who inspired thousands of people to reach their potential and become the best they could be would not be coming to a poor widow, looking for revenge for something her deceased husband did.

Yeah, okay, five minutes ago I was just someone who used to know Rick, but I wasn't above playing the poor widow card if it got me out of a mess Rick's dealings got me into.

"I'm Bryan Kollar." He held out a large, muscular hand.

I accepted his handshake, pleased to see my fingers weren't shaking, and was surprised he didn't try to squash my hand. I guess if you're really strong, you don't have to prove it.

"Were you a friend of Rick's?" I asked. Might as well get the ugly stuff out there on the table.

"No."

"An enemy?"

His smile widened. Did I mention he was really nice to look at? "No, I'm not a friend or an enemy. We were business associates."

Uh oh. *Business* with Rick usually meant a scam. What on earth was he thinking about, trying to swindle a man with wealth and power and the ability to break him in two with one hand?

"What kind of business?" I asked warily.

He shrugged, the simple gesture sending those mounds of muscles in his chest and arms rippling. I wondered what I could say to make him shrug again.

"A real estate deal."

Of course it was. Rick was a commercial real estate salesman. He did real estate deals regularly. Some were even legitimate.

"Your husband purchased some property from my elderly parents," Bryan continued. "They're..." He looked very sad. I wanted to comfort him. He sighed. "I'm afraid they're becoming a little senile. They should never have sold him the property in the first place. It's worthless, an old flour mill that's been owned by my family for four generations."

Rick didn't think the property was worthless or he wouldn't have bought it, but I waited for the rest of the story.

"My parents are now very upset that they sold it to him. They're elderly and susceptible, and I think your husband kind of bullied them in a charming sort of way until they finally agreed."

"Rick could pour on the charm when he needed to," I admitted. *Just like you're doing to me right now.*

"Your husband and I were negotiating a deal where I would buy back the property for my parents. We had a verbal agreement that I'd pay him a price that was twice what he paid for the property." The wide smile returned. Somehow that smile wasn't as pretty as it had been before.

I waited a moment for him to continue. He didn't. "And you're telling me this, why?"

"You are his only surviving heir, aren't you? He told me how he lost his parents in that horrible plane crash."

I gave a jerky nod, trying to remember if I'd heard the plane crash story. There were so many versions of his family history. "Yes, as far as I know, I'm his only surviving heir." I suddenly realized that meant I'd get custody not only of any bits and pieces of his body that the cops found but also of his estate. I did not want that. "I'll be happy to return your parents' property to you for whatever price Rick paid for it as soon as I'm legally able to do so."

Bryan's smile went off the charts again. I'd just made the man very happy. I felt certain this deal had little to do with his parents and a whole lot to do with his bank account, but I didn't care. I wanted nothing to do with Rick's deals or his property. I'd be happy to give him back his family's old flour mill.

Bryan's gaze shifted to something behind me.

I turned and saw that Paula had come in. She was frowning. "Lindsay? What's going on?"

"Paula, this is Bryan Kollar, the owner of those Body by Bryan gyms. Mr. Kollar, this is Paula Roberts."

"Please, it's Bryan. Mr. Kollar sounds so formal. Nice to meet you, Paula." Bryan extended his hand.

Paula stepped forward and shook his hand briefly. She wasn't smiling. "Nice to meet you, Mr. Kollar."

24

Okay, there was definitely something she didn't like about this man.

He didn't seem to notice. He continued to exude charm and affability. He pulled a slim wallet from his back pocket (I had no idea how he managed that feat considering how tight those pants were) and extracted a couple of cards. "You can reach me at any of these numbers. If I'm not there, leave a message and I'll get right back to you." He flipped the cards over and laid them on the counter. "And on the back is a gift certificate for a free workout and tour at any of my facilities."

My smile was becoming more forced all the time. I actually found that a little tacky, giving us a *gift certificate* obviously intended to be a promotion for business. But all those manners my mother taught me kicked over in automatic mode. I grabbed a napkin, reached inside the glass case on the counter and withdrew one of my famous chocolate chip cookies.

"Thank you," I said. "Please accept a gift from my business too." I offered him the cookie.

He stepped backward and looked slightly alarmed as if I'd just offered him a gift of smallpox. He maintained his smile, but it was starting to look really strained. "No, thank you."

Well, that was awkward. Maybe he had allergies. I laid down the cookie and picked up a brownie. "Gluten free, no nuts."

He shook his head. "I appreciate the offer, but I don't eat sugar, refined flour or chocolate. Those things are all toxic to your body."

I felt as if I'd been slapped. "Well, then, how about a Coke for the road? A little high fructose corn syrup, caffeine and artificial coloring?" I grabbed a glass, filled it with foaming brown liquid from the fountain, and slammed it onto the counter, sloshing some out.

He looked at the mess on the counter then back up to me. He no longer looked pretty. "I'm sorry for your loss," he said, the words plastic. "I'll be in touch." He left.

"I can't believe he did that!" Paula exclaimed.

"Me neither! How can anybody turn down my cookies and brownies and call them toxic? The man's insane!"

"He's certainly rude, coming around here to try to get something from you the day after Rick dies. That's just wrong. You should not sell him that property, Lindsay. I don't trust him. That property's valuable. He's trying to take advantage of your grief, catch you when you're vulnerable."

I picked up the discarded cookie and took a bite. "Let's don't start believing the official version of the story. I'm not grieving, and I'm not vulnerable."

Paula took the glass of Coke and pitched the contents before I could stop her then began cleaning the counter. "Yes, you are. You don't want to admit it, but you are."

Why did everybody except Fred and Henry think I was secretly upset about Rick?

"Let's agree to disagree on that one, but it has nothing to do with my selling him that property he wants. You know Rick finagled it away from Kollar's parents. That's what Rick does! He cons people into selling when they don't want to, into letting him have property for pennies on the dollar. I want nothing to do with that old flour mill or anything else Rick's been involved in. I don't want to be his heir. I don't want to get a box containing two vertebrae and an ear. I don't want to inherit his sleazy land deals or that house where he lived with Muffy and Becky and who knows who else?"

"Give it all to charity."

I considered that. "The vertebrae and the ear too?"

She arched an eyebrow. "No."

We both burst into giggles.

The front door opened and a woman strode in looking regal even in tight blue jeans and a blouse cut too low for anything except a Playboy photo shoot. She was followed by two tall, well-built men, her retinue. The woman was beautiful in spite of having a little too much of everything...blond hair, makeup and boobs. The men were either her sons or her brothers as they bore a striking resemblance to her except for not having excess blond hair, makeup and boobs.

"I'm sorry," Paula said. "We're closed."

The woman rushed across the room toward us. Damn! Were we about to be robbed? I should have pushed Trent harder to let me get a gun.

"You must be my darling Lindsay," she gushed, grabbing Paula's hands and trying to pull her across the counter.

Eyes wide with shock, Paula shoved against the woman. "Get away from me!"

I knew Paula wasn't her darling Lindsay, and while my name might be Lindsay, I was just as sure I wasn't her darling. Nevertheless, I spoke up.

"Leave her alone! I'm Lindsay. Who are you? What do you want?"

The woman turned her attention to me. I stepped backward, out of her reach. She spread her arms wide. "Lindsay, sweetheart, I'm your mother!"

I was not expecting that. "No, you're not my mother. I've met my mother, and you're definitely not my mother."

She gave a coy smile. "I'm Rick's mother, so I'm your mother-in-law, and these are your brothers!" She turned and swept a hand in the direction of the two men.

Chapter Five

"Please have a seat," Paula said with a sweeping gesture outward, indicating the room full of empty tables. I silently blessed her for keeping her calm while I was stricken dumb...and I mean that in both definitions of the word. "Someone will be with you in a moment," she continued.

Okay, maybe she wasn't completely rational either. More like acting out of habit. When someone came in the door, she told them to be seated then took their order. But at least she was doing something. That was more than I could say about myself. I was in total shock. Sure, I knew Rick had lied to me about his family. All the contradictory stories couldn't be true, so after a while I'd put the whole thing out of my mind. His family didn't exist.

These three people certainly existed in a larger-than-life way.

Paula hurried across the room to put up the "Closed" sign. I hoped she didn't lock the door in case I needed to escape quickly.

"I wish we didn't have to meet under such sad circumstances," Rick's new-found mother said.

I licked my dry lips. "Let's, uh, sit down and, uh, get acquainted." I repeated Paula's gesture toward the room of tables and chairs. I wasn't coming out from around that counter until they moved away. I didn't want to risk being grabbed.

"Yes," Paula said, returning to my side. "Everybody sit down, and I'll bring you something to drink and some of Lindsay's famous chocolate desserts." Still acting the part of the perfect waitress.

The boys ambled toward the closest table and sat. "I'd like coffee, if you got some made," one of them said.

"Me too, with cream," the other one said.

Mama remained at the counter, smiling and waiting. She reminded me of a tarantula who'd spotted her prey and wasn't going to let it get away.

I sidled around the counter, plotting a circuitous path toward the table where the boys sat. It was a futile attempt. I'd barely made it around the counter when Mama grabbed me, wrapping me in a stranglehold embrace of such intensity I thought she must work out at one of Bryan's gyms. Her perfume was even stronger than her embrace. I wasn't sure if I was going to be strangled or suffocated.

"I know just how you feel," she said, patting my back and dragging me toward the table. I refrained from saying I seriously doubted she had any idea how I felt unless she'd been accosted by a boa constrictor who smelled like a service station bathroom. "I lost Rick's father when he was a baby." She looked sad or something remotely resembling sad. "That was bad enough, but at least he wasn't murdered like our poor Rick."

I flopped into a chair and drew in a deep breath, grateful to escape from Mama's tentacles.

30

She took my hand between both of hers. I was afraid to try to move it, afraid I'd slice off a finger on one of her inch-long red nails.

Paula appeared with three coffees, one Coke and assorted chocolate goodies.

Mama had to let go of me to pick up her cup. "This is excellent coffee," she said, leaving a huge red lipstick print on the cup and smiling up at Paula. Between Bryan and this group, there sure was a lot of artificial smiling going on around the place that day.

I motioned with my eyes for Paula to join us. Well, that's what I tried to do. At first she looked a little confused, even concerned, as if my eye rolling meant I was having a seizure of some sort. Finally she caught on, pulled over a chair and sat down between me and the brothers.

"I'm Paula Roberts," she said. "I don't believe I caught your names."

Mama fluttered a hand at her throat. "How rude of me. I just felt so much like family as soon as I saw my darling Lindsay, I completely forgot we'd never actually met. I'm Marissa Malone." She looked at me and reached for me again. I grabbed a Coke with one hand and a cookie with the other so she could only pat my arm. "But you can call me Mother." Big smile.

"I, uh…"

"Nice to meet you, Marissa," Paula said.

"These are Rick's brothers, Clint and Brad." She indicated the boys.

"Clint and Brad…Kramer or Malone?" Paula asked.

Marissa smiled. "Clint West and Brad Parker."

The boys nodded politely. And smiled, of course.

My mind was spinning, trying to take it all in. "So you're Rick's half-brothers? You have different fathers?" All three of them looked enough like Rick that I didn't for one minute doubt her story of their relationship. Blue eyes, dark blond hair with streaks of lighter blond, strong nose, arrogant expression. I was actually surprised to find the boys were only half-siblings.

Marissa smiled and dipped her eyelashes. "Same father. We all just decided to take new names after their daddy left. Get rid of bad memories."

I resisted the impulse to ask if that was the same father who died when Rick was a baby. At least I could see where Rick got his trait of making up family history.

"I understand about bad memories," I said. Like the ones we were making at that very moment.

"These are good cookies," Clint said.

"Yeah," Brad agreed. "You're a good cook."

"Thank you." At least they were telling the truth about that.

"So you heard about Rick's death?" Paula asked.

"Yes." Marissa set down her cup. I leaned backward in Paula's direction, away from Marissa, clutching Coke and cookies and trying to avoid the possibility of more grabbing or patting. "As soon as we heard about Rick's terrible death, we made plans to get here and help out with whatever we can." She gave me another sorrowful look, and I scooted farther away.

Somehow I doubted Marissa's assertion that they'd come to help. Maybe to help themselves to

Rick's possessions. Missouri's a community property state so I was entitled to half of everything Rick and I owned, but unless he left a Will, since he had no offspring his heirs-at-law were entitled to the other half of his estate. Well, they were welcome to it. Obviously Rick had been dodging them for years so he probably wouldn't want them to have it, and that made the deal even sweeter. It would give me a lot of pleasure to hand over his prized possessions to people he didn't like.

"I just can't imagine why anyone would want to hurt my son." She pulled a tissue from her purse and dabbed at her dry eyes.

I could think of at least seven or twelve reasons why someone would want to hurt Rick, but I decided to let that one go. "Where do you all live?" I asked. They had to be fairly close or they wouldn't have heard about Rick's death. I was pretty sure he didn't make the national news.

Marissa's expression grew a little vague for a moment then cleared as she said, "St. Louis."

"Wow. So you've been living four hours away all these years, and you never visited before?"

Marissa lowered her gaze, fluttering her long lashes that absolutely did not grow out of her eyelids. "We had a silly little fight." She lifted her gaze to mine again. "And you know how stubborn Rick can be."

"Yes," I said, "I do know that." Missouri-mule stubborn, determined, obstinate. Almost as stubborn as I am.

She shook her head. "I always thought we'd reconcile and be together as a family some time. It never occurred to me that he might…" She paused to choke out a half-sob as phony as her eyelashes. "I never thought he might die. He was so young."

"It was tragic," Paula said. I looked at her, and she gave a slight shrug. I just wanted to be sure she didn't really believe what she said.

"Well," I said, "it was really nice to meet you all. I'm sure I'll see you again."

"Of course you will. We're family, and we're here to help arrange for my son's funeral."

Something else they were welcome to, his funeral. I had no desire to participate in that little festivity. "Okay. I'll call the police department and have them ship the remains to you instead of to me. Where are you staying?"

"Oh, dear," Marissa said. "I'm afraid that's going to be a problem." Her features settled into lines of distress and she wrung her hands. I'd never seen anybody wring their hands before. Even my mother, with her penchant for dramatics, had never wrung her hands.

"Why is that going to be a problem?" I asked, though I had a bad feeling I could guess the answer.

"We planned to stay in my son's house."

I rather liked that image, Rick's estranged family in his house, his mother sleeping where his bimbos had slept, his brothers putting their dirty shoes on the expensive sofa. He'd had that house professionally decorated when we moved in and was very proud of it.

"But we drove by there, and the police have it roped off with that awful yellow tape."

"Oh, yes, the awful yellow tape. I'm sure it'll be down in a day or two."

Marissa lifted a manicured hand to her throat and smiled. "Oh, thank goodness! And until we can get into Rick's house, you don't mind if we stay with you, do you?"

Of course I minded! I did not want those people anywhere near my house.

"I have a very small place," I said, trying to wiggle out of that awful possibility without being blunt and rude.

Marissa frowned. "You do? But your family's rich."

Okay, that was weird. "My family's not rich," I assured her, "and it wouldn't matter if they were. I have a small house."

"Your daddy's a lawyer."

Where did she get this information? Obviously she'd been checking up on me. "Yeah, but he's not rich, and what does that have to do with me anyway?" I liked these people less and less with every word out of that woman's mouth.

"Rick's house has five bedrooms."

She certainly had her facts in order. "Yes, it does, and that has nothing to do with me. I have just enough room for me and my cat, and he sheds a lot. Even people without allergies to cats are allergic to my cat. You wouldn't be comfortable there. Just give it a couple of days and you'll be able to get into Rick's house with its five bedrooms, plush carpeting, no cats, no dogs." *If you don't mind a few bits and pieces of Rick hanging around in the flower beds.* "I know someone on the police department. Let me call and see how long they plan to keep his place roped off."

Marissa's eyes widened. "You know a cop?"

I decided it probably wasn't the right time to tell her that her son's death meant I was officially dating that cop.

"Excuse me. I'll go make that call." I stood then looked back at Paula. I didn't want to leave her alone with Mama and the boys. "Can you come help me?" I asked.

She frowned but rose and followed me to the kitchen. "Help you what?" she whispered. "Have you forgotten how to make a phone call?"

"I didn't think you'd want to be out there alone with them."

She shrugged. "I can handle it. I'd better go back. I'd hate for them to steal the tables and chairs when we weren't looking."

I nodded. "They might. They are Rick's family."

"Yes."

She went back out, and I called Trent on my cell phone. He wasn't in, of course. Probably out there somewhere giving tickets to innocent speeders. I did get hold of Lawson, however. "When are you taking down that awful yellow tape?" I asked. "Rick's mother is here, and she wants to stay in his house, but if she can't, she wants to stay in mine!"

He was silent for a moment. Anybody else would have asked me to elaborate, but Lawson just mulled it over until he got a handle on my rantings. "We should be finished in another day or two."

"A day or two? No, I need you to be more precise. In fact, I need you to take down that tape right now and let these people in there. What's the big deal, anyway? The crime happened in the driveway, not in the house. There aren't going to be any body parts in the house."

"But there may be evidence."

"You've had twenty-four hours to get that evidence out of there. Why is it taking so long to fingerprint a few glasses and check for sex videos? It never takes that long on television."

"This isn't television."

"If you don't get that tape down so these people can stay there, I'm going to drop them off on your front porch."

It was, of course, an empty threat. I didn't even know where Lawson lived.

He was silent for several moments. "I'll see what I can do, but tomorrow's going to be the earliest possible time."

I sighed. "I suppose that's better than *a day or two*. Thank you."

I went back out to find Clint and Brad laying the charm on Paula. I could have told them they were wasting their expertise. After being married to an abusive jerk who tried to kill me, send her to prison and take her son from her, Paula's learned to look out for herself. She does a great imitation of a turtle, just goes inside her shell while her lips continue to smile.

"You can probably get into Rick's house tomorrow," I said. "I'll help you find a nice motel for tonight."

Marissa burst into tears. Her sons jumped up from their seats and came around to comfort her.

"I just can't stand the thought of a lonely motel room with my son dead!" she wailed.

"It's okay, Mama. We'll take care of you." Clint patted her shoulder and glared at me. His glare was enough like Rick's that it didn't bother me in the slightest. I'd become immune over the years.

"I thought we could comfort each other," Marissa said before she settled back into disconsolate weeping.

"Don't cry, Mama." Brad did his best to glare me down too. "My brother's got to be rolling in his grave right now."

"I don't think so. He's not in his grave yet." I refrained from adding that, with his body in ten bazillion pieces, he probably wasn't going to be rolling around a lot anyway.

Marissa's hand shot out and grabbed mine, her tear-filled eyes imploring me. "You're not a mother, so you don't know how awful it is to lose a son, especially in such a horrible way. I need to be with family to get through this night."

I knew she was scamming me. I knew she wasn't really upset about Rick's death and I wasn't really family. But, just like Rick used to do, she was wearing me down. I was tired of hearing it. I didn't want to argue. And, of course, there were all those manners my mother had force fed me for so many years they'd become automatic.

I threw my hands into the air. "Fine. You can all stay at my place, but I only have one guest room with one double bed. Somebody's going to have to sleep on the sofa, and it's not going to be me or my cat."

Chapter Six

Mama and the boys followed me to my house. The scam business must be booming. They were driving a shiny new Cadillac. Or maybe they stole it. Not that I had any reason to think they were car thieves. Rick had never stolen a car. That would be too upfront and simple. More fun to scam people out of their vehicles and their property.

I made a mental note of the license plate so I could call Fred and have him check it for me.

By the time I got my older model (but still fast) Celica settled in my detached garage that looked as if it might topple over at any minute, Mama and the boys were waiting on my front porch with their luggage. Designer luggage. The scam business was obviously more profitable than a chocolate shop.

"This is different from where Rick lives," Marissa said, sounding disappointed as she looked around at the neighborhood, taking in Fred's meticulous lawn and house, the unkempt vacant house across the street, Paula's ordinary yard and, of course, my organic, pesticide-free, fertilizer-free, weed-killer-free, mostly grass-free yard.

"Yes," I said, turning the key in my front door lock. "Rick and I are very different people."

"What a pretty cat!" Marissa said as I opened the door. She bent down and reached for Henry. He laid his ears back, arched his back, spit and hissed at her then swiped at her hand with one paw. She screamed and jerked away.

"Be careful," I cautioned. "He's part mountain lion." Yes, that was an outrageous lie, but she started it. *Come to help out with whatever we can.* Give me a break!

Henry kept his distance, making it obvious he didn't like the new guests. He slunk around, a series of growling sounds coming from deep in his throat. Feline cursing. This confirmed that these people were related to Rick. Henry had always given him that same treatment.

"The guest room is upstairs." I indicated the stairs then waved a hand toward my big, cushy sofa patterned with lots of brightly colored flowers. "One of you can sleep here." I then indicated the hardwood floor on the other side of the coffee table. "And one of you can sleep here." Yes, I could have offered to borrow an air mattress from Fred, but I saw no reason to try to make my unwelcome guests comfortable. Even the manners my mother instilled in me have some limitations.

Brad and Clint exchanged disappointed glances. Marissa smiled tightly. "We'll make do with whatever you can offer. We do so appreciate your hospitality, and it means so much to be with someone else who loved Rick."

I decided to let that last comment pass unchallenged, though if they knew so much about me, I was pretty sure they'd know it wasn't true.

I led them upstairs to my guest room with its small antique bed that barely held a double sized mattress. Marissa's smile got even tighter, but she set her bags down. "Where is the guest bath?"

"Down the hall. It's the guest bath and the master bath all in one. When this house was built, indoor plumbing was considered an extravagance. Nobody even thought about having more than one bathroom."

"Thank you so much. We'll be just fine, won't we, boys?"

"Yes, Mama," they both mumbled. I could tell they weren't at all certain they were going to be just fine.

"While you get settled in, I need to feed my cat. If he doesn't get his dinner on time, he's been known to attack the nearest food source." I looked pointedly at Marissa's tanned arm that Henry had lashed out at already. She nodded vaguely. I think she wasn't sure whether to believe me but decided it best to err on the side of caution.

I went downstairs and filled Henry's food bowl. I debated whether to give him some catnip. He loves that particular herb, and it would alleviate his anxiety about having those people in his home. But I didn't trust Rick's relations. I needed Henry on full alert, my guard cat. He'd just have to tough it out and get through the evening sober.

Henry finished his food and asked to go outside. I opened the back door. "You're on curfew tonight," I warned him. "Be home before dark."

41

He looked up at me, gave a short meow and slipped out the door. He'd be back when he got good and ready. We both knew it.

My phone rang, the landline. I cringed. My mother always called on that line. She refused to have anything to do with "those awful cell phones that can give you brain cancer." And it didn't matter if the cell phone was only on the other end.

I really didn't want to talk to her at that moment. Or any moment in the next few hours, for that matter. But I lifted the receiver. "Hello?"

"Are you all right?"

Fred. I breathed a sigh of relief.

"I'm fine. Why wouldn't I be?"

"You're not answering your cell phone, and there's a car sitting in front of your house that's rented by a woman who doesn't exist."

Silly me, thinking I'd have to ask Fred to find out about Marissa's Cadillac. "Couldn't hear the cell phone over the people talking, and that woman definitely exists, just probably under another name. Or several other names."

"Marissa Malone?"

I laughed. "Yeah. Rick's mom."

"Rick's mother?" I'd finally managed to surprise Fred.

"Who knows what her real name is? She and Rick's two brothers changed their names after dear old Dad departed."

"Brothers?" I loved it. He was totally confused. "Rick's father really is dead, not in prison somewhere?"

42

"You know all those lies Rick told me about his family? Seems he had good reason to keep them hidden. I don't know if Dad's dead or just hiding from Mom. Guess it doesn't matter. He's gone somewhere, as opposed to the rest of the family who are right here in my house."

"What are they doing at your house?"

"Spending the night." I sighed. "They planned to stay at Rick's house, but it's got that awful yellow tape all around it."

"Yeah, the cops have a habit of doing that when somebody gets blown to bits. I don't like the idea of their staying with you."

"Neither do I and neither does Henry. But it should be just the one night. I talked to Lawson, and he's going to try to get Rick's house released tomorrow."

"Are you sure they're really Rick's family members?"

"Probably. They look like him, and Henry reacts to them the same way he reacts to Rick. They're here to grab his estate, and I'm more than happy to let them have it, whoever they are."

"You'll be leaving at four in the morning to go to work. Are you going to leave them alone in your house?"

I thought about that for a moment. "No. They'll be leaving at four o'clock too."

"Let me know if you need anything."

"Thanks, I will."

"I mean it. Anything. Like a mad man coming through the door with a machine gun."

I burst into laughter, remembering when I'd asked Fred to do that to get rid of Rick, never expecting he really would. He really did.

I hung up then went into the living room to retrieve my cell phone from my purse where I'd left it on the coffee table.

Mama was sitting on the sofa between the two boys while Brad flipped through the channels on my nineteen inch TV.

"No cable?" he asked.

Further proof this was Rick's family.

I waved a hand at the built-in oak bookcase that covered most of one wall of the room. "I have plenty of reading material."

The boys looked at each other then at their mother as if for guidance about what to do in such a strange situation.

She smiled. Of course she did. "Let's sit down and talk. We have so many plans to make, the funeral and everything."

I sat in the recliner and checked my cell phone. Five calls from Fred and three from Trent. I needed to call Trent back, but I might as well get this conversation with Marissa out of the way first. It wouldn't take long.

"Do whatever you want about the funeral," I said. "If he hadn't been killed, Rick and I would be divorced. I'd have this house, Paula's rental house next door, my restaurant and all accounts that are in my name only. Unless he left a Will, and I can't imagine that he did since he thought he'd live forever, all the rest is yours."

Marissa blinked rapidly a couple of times. "I see," she said, her voice a couple of octaves lower than it had been before. "However, as his wife, you're entitled to half of his estate even if he didn't leave a Will."

"I'm entitled to *my* half of *our* estate. But I told you what I want. Take everything else and welcome to it."

For the first time, Marissa really smiled. So did her sons. The atmosphere lightened considerably.

"Okay," I said, "let's order a pizza, have dinner, then go to bed. I have to be at the restaurant at four o'clock in the morning, and we're all leaving when I leave because I have to set the security system." No, I didn't have a security system, but it sounded like a good excuse for getting them out and keeping them out.

"Order a pizza? You don't cook?" Clint asked. "You have a restaurant, and you don't cook?"

"I make chocolate desserts. If you'd like brownies for dinner, I can fix you right up. Otherwise, we'll have pizza."

His mother patted his leg, and he shut up.

I picked up my cell phone to call in the pizza order, but it rang before I had a chance to hit the speed dial. I didn't recognize the number, but it wasn't blocked like a sales call so I answered.

"Lindsay, it's Bryan Kollar."

Like I wouldn't recognize that compelling baritone voice from his commercials. Even though I'd decided I didn't much like the guy, I could have listened to that voice for at least an hour or two. Maybe he was descended from one of the Sirens.

"Yes, Bryan. What can I do for you?" In the siege of relatives, I'd forgotten about my earlier conversation with Beautiful Bryan. I had my hands and my house full at the moment and didn't really want to deal with him, exquisite voice notwithstanding.

"If you have a minute—"

"I don't, actually," I said, interrupting him. Rude of me, I know. My mother would be mortified. "I'm in the middle of something, very tied up right now."

"No problem. I can come by your restaurant tomorrow."

"What? No. Why would you do that?"

"I took the liberty of having my attorney draw up some papers about our intent to do business," he said smoothly.

"Oh, yeah. Your parents' property. About that, I don't know if I can sign those papers—"

"You said it wouldn't be a problem, that you'd be happy to return the property to me." He interrupted me that time. We were even.

"I said I'd give it back to you as soon as I'm legally able to do so. Well, something's come up, and I may not be legally able to give you back that property."

"What's come up? Why wouldn't you be able to give me back that property?" His voice was no longer so compelling. In fact, it had become downright scary. Threatening.

"Turns out Rick's family didn't die in that horrible plane crash after all. His mother and two brothers are sitting right here in my living room." I kept my gaze focused on the floor. I should have gone into the kitchen to take the call.

"I see," Bryan said.

"Okay, look, I'll get back to you when we get this sorted out."

"May I come over and talk to Mrs. Kramer?"

"Not tonight."

"When?"

My phone beeped. A call coming in from Trent.

"I'll get back to you as soon as I can set up something. Gotta go now. Cops are on the other line."

I accepted Trent's call, cutting Bryan off.

"It's about time," he said. "I was getting worried. I'm on my way over there."

"By all means, come on. Party's at my place. BYOP, bring your own pizza."

"I can do that. What's this Lawson's telling me about Rick's mother and brothers arriving in town?"

"Oh, yeah. We'll discuss that later."

"Later? Why? Are they there now?"

"Oh, yeah."

"At your house?"

"Oh, yeah."

"For the night?"

"Oh, yeah."

"I don't like that. They may be imposters."

"Yeah, that's possible. I don't really care."

He gave a long sigh. "His former wife and son who came into the station today may be imposters too."

Chapter Seven

"I didn't mean to eavesdrop," Marissa said when I hung up, "but I couldn't help overhearing your conversation." I resisted the urge to tell her that polite manners dictated when you accidentally overheard something, you were supposed to pretend you hadn't. I didn't think Marissa would be interested in learning manners at that late date. "Who is Bryan and what property are you talking about giving back to him?"

I really wished she'd sit there and be quiet and give me a chance to wrap my brain around this latest news. An ex-wife? A son? I'd learned more about Rick in the twenty-four hours since his death than in the five years I was married to him. But I shoved those thoughts to the back of my mind and explained the Bryan situation to Marissa.

"So this was a piece of property Rick bought as an investment?" She'd gone from simpering lady to shrewd real estate investor.

"I suppose. I really don't know any of the details. If it was up to me, I'd sell the property back to Kollar's family, but it's probably going to be up to you what you do with it."

She nodded. "I'd like to find out what Rick planned to do with it."

"We may never know." That should keep her up half the night.

She smiled. "Oh, I'm sure we'll find something. Did he have a computer?"

"He had a laptop he took everywhere with him. It probably got blown up in the explosion."

She pondered that. Her smile slipped briefly but then returned. "When we get into his house, we'll find out."

I had a feeling if she couldn't figure out what Rick had planned to do with the property, she'd come up with an alternative plan for it, one that would bring her a lot of money and leave Bryan's parents sucking wind.

After what seemed like an eternity of trying to make small talk with Marissa, I was rescued by Trent's arrival with a pizza. I greeted him at the door. "Thank goodness you're here."

"Are you that hungry?"

"No."

Henry appeared like a ghost from out of the gathering dusk and strolled inside with Trent.

I shut the door behind the two guys and turned to my uninvited guests. "This is my boyfriend," I said, no longer caring if the Malone/West/Parker contingency thought I had been immoral by seeing another man while still legally tied to their worthless son and brother. "Marissa Malone, Clint West, Brad Parker, this is Adam Trent. Detective Adam Trent of the Pleasant Grove Police Department." I'd told them a friend was coming with pizza. I waited until he got there to tell them he was a cop so we could observe their initial reactions together. That's what romance is all about, sharing the little things.

Marissa paled but still managed a smile. The boys rose to shake hands. Trent set the pizza on the coffee table and accepted their hands in turn. We were all so polite.

I went to the kitchen and returned with Cokes, paper plates and paper towels.

"Are you investigating my son's murder?" Marissa asked.

"Not officially," Trent replied.

Because of his relationship with me, he wasn't officially involved, but I knew he was smack dab in the middle of it. Marissa didn't need to know that information.

We ate pizza in silence for a few minutes. Henry sat in the corner of the room, watching every movement, occasionally switching his tail. He takes his guard cat duties seriously. Or he was waiting for somebody to drop a bit of pizza. Whatever.

After everybody set their empty plates and Coke cans on the coffee table, I rose to gather them up and take them to the kitchen, but Trent stopped me. "I'll do that. You brought it all in. You just sit there and relax."

He put the plates and napkins inside the empty box then carefully picked up all the Coke cans by the bent tabs, set them on the box and took everything to the kitchen. I knew what he was doing. I'd been a cop's almost-girlfriend long enough to know a few things. He'd take the cans in and have them fingerprinted, find out exactly who we were dealing with.

He came back and resumed his seat in the armchair. "So you folks drove in from St. Louis?" he asked. He was doing the Mr. Stone Face cop thing. I felt a happy tingle. Mama and the boys were in trouble.

"Yes," she said.

"Just got in town today?"

"That's right."

"What part of St. Louis do you live in?"

Marissa shifted slightly on the sofa. "We don't exactly live there right now. We move around a lot."

"Demands of your job?"

"Yes, we have a small real estate company, and we move from town to town depending on the availability of properties."

Aha! No wonder Rick was so good at what he did. He'd learned it growing up in the family business.

I suspected Mama and the boys moved from town to town in order to avoid being lynched after they scammed somebody.

"When did you get to Kansas City?"

It suddenly dawned on me that Trent was trying to determine if she had an alibi for the time of the murder! Well, he'd asked me. Why shouldn't he ask her?

Marissa wasn't new to this game. She gave him a crimped smile. "We got here just after noon today. As I said, we drove in from St. Louis. We were staying with friends there who'll be happy to verify that we were with them all day yesterday."

Trent nodded. "I see. Ever been to Crappie Creek?"

51

For anyone not familiar with fish, it's pronounced croppy, not crappy, but I think either pronunciation is appropriate for that small, desolate town in southern Missouri.

Marissa flinched when he said the name. She'd obviously been there. For a moment she said nothing as if deciding whether to lie or tell the truth. I had no doubt if she hadn't known Trent was a cop, she'd have opted for lying. Finally she gave a broad smile. "Of course I've been there. All my boys were born there."

Rick had claimed various cities as his place of birth—Dallas, New York, London, Los Angeles, Houston—but Crappie Creek had never made the list. I almost regretted that Rick was dead. I would have loved to be able to throw all these new-found truths in his face, confront him with his lies.

I tried to share a *gotcha* glance with Trent, but he kept his gaze focused on his target. "Did you know Grace Ganyon when you lived in Crappie Creek?"

Red crept up Marissa's neck and suffused her face. Her jaw tightened though she never lost her smile. It just began to look more like a grimace than a smile. "It's a small town. Everybody knows everybody. Of course I know Grace."

"And her son Rickie?"

Marissa gave up her attempt to appear amiable. She glowered. "That boy is not Rick's son."

Well. She certainly knew about the boy.

"But Rick and Grace were married when the child was born?" Trent asked.

"Married?" Marissa snorted. "That's what she told people, but my son would never marry trash like her, and that boy is not his." Marissa tilted her nose upward as if in scorn.

Trent folded his arms and studied her quietly for a few moments. "They're planning to move into Rick's house too. Good thing there are five bedrooms."

Marissa shot to her feet. "I refuse to let that woman stay in my son's house!"

Trent shrugged and looked at me. He was still being Mr. Stone Face, but his eyes were glowing with green sparks. He was enjoying this. "Actually, it's not up to you who stays in Rick's house. Lindsay's name is on the title of that house. Until her husband's estate is settled, she's in charge of what happens to it."

Marissa sat back down and smiled at me.

I returned her smile, and mine was genuine as I contemplated what fun it would be to put Rick's mother, brothers, ex-wife and possible son all together in his house. I'd have to go for a visit. Take a video. Share it with Fred and Paula. Maybe post it on the Internet.

Trent rose. "I'd better be going. I know how early Lindsay has to get up. It was nice to meet you folks. Lindsay, could I trouble you for a couple of cookies to go?"

He followed me to the kitchen where he waved a hand at the empty Coke cans. "I didn't want to alert them to what I'm doing. Have you got a bag I can hide these in?"

I gave him a white plastic grocery store bag. "You don't think they'll be suspicious when your sack of cookies rattles?"

He grinned. "I'll tell them they're stale cookies." He started out of the kitchen then turned back, his expression serious. "You probably need to hire a lawyer to get Rick's estate straightened out."

"I suppose so. Maybe Dad will step in. They have a probate lawyer at their firm. Dying isn't as disreputable as getting a divorce."

"That would be good. If I were you, I'd request a DNA test on the son."

"We'll see. As long as I get what's mine, I don't care if the rest of his estate goes to some alcoholic bum living under a bridge."

"Marissa's going to fight that boy's claim."

"If that really is his son, I guess he's entitled to something. Rick didn't pay any child support. At least, not that I know of. Heck, I don't know anything about what he did or who he was." I gave a resigned sigh. "Okay, I'll talk to a lawyer and get all that stuff set up."

Trent said good night to Mama and the boys, and I walked out on the porch with him. He wrapped his arms around me and gave me a long, delicious kiss. I melted against him. Well, almost. Even though it was dark and there was no way Rick could be watching, when some animal rattled in the bushes, I gasped and jumped back, searching the shadows for signs of Rickhead.

Trent smiled, but his gaze darted around involuntarily. He shared my paranoia. "As soon as you get rid of your house full of company—" He finished the sentence with another kiss.

The critter in the bushes made a hissing noise as if objecting to our embrace. Which, I told myself,

54

was not possible. I was pretty sure the wild animals didn't care if I kissed Trent.

"Possum," I said. "I'll turn Henry out and he'll take care of it. Then tomorrow…" I gave him what I hoped was a seductive smile.

"Tomorrow."

He left and I went back inside to spend the night with Mama and the boys.

Chapter Eight

The next morning I dashed into the kitchen at Death by Chocolate thirty minutes late. Paula was already up to her elbows in cinnamon roll dough. "I'm sorry," I said, setting my purse down and preparing to make chocolate at record speed.

"I was getting worried," she said, sprinkling sugar and cinnamon onto her sheet of dough.

"I just couldn't get those people moving. Took Mama half an hour to put on her makeup. I really think they believed if they dallied long enough, I was going to let them stay there all day. Like Henry would have tolerated that." I tied an industrial strength apron over my jeans and T-shirt and scrubbed my hands in the big sink. "You should have heard Brad whine when the hot water ran out before he finished his shower! That kind of made it all worthwhile."

"You should have told him there was plenty of hot water at the Motel Six down the street."

I laughed. "They ought to be able to get in Rick's house today, and I'll be rid of them. And you'll never guess who else is going to be staying in Rick's house. His ex-wife and son!"

Paula's jaw dropped, and she stopped halfway through rolling up the cinnamon dough. "Ex-wife? Son? Rick was married before? He has a son?"

I brought out my mixing bowl and prepared to begin the chocolate. "Well, Marissa says they weren't really married and that the boy isn't Rick's, so who knows what the truth is? We'll see. I'm going to call Dad and see if he can set me up with a probate lawyer so we can get everything straightened out. Probably need to get a DNA test on the boy. If Rick left a Will, this is going to get even more interesting. If he did, I'm sure none of those people are in it and all of them will challenge it."

Paula went back to rolling up the dough. "You ought to get DNA tests on all of them."

I shrugged. "I have no doubt that woman is really Rick's mother, and those boys look an awful lot like him. But I might insist on tests for everybody just for fun if they keep annoying me."

"Where are they now?"

"I have no idea. I drove here as fast as I could, hoping they wouldn't follow me."

She gave me a skeptical look. "They found you yesterday."

And they found me again that day. A few minutes after we put up the *Open* sign, Mama and the boys came in and seated themselves at a table near the window.

I fed them and resisted the urge to present them with a bill. How tacky would that be? But I was tempted.

The breakfast crowd thinned, and Paula and I began preparations for lunch. I was making Cookie

Dough Cheesecake Bars, and Paula was chopping ham when the kitchen door burst open.

"Can I help you do something?" Marissa asked cheerfully.

I cringed at the mere thought of her being involved in our food. "No, thanks," I said. "We've got it all under control."

She stepped further into the room, letting the doors swing closed behind her. "Are you sure? You've done so much for us, we'd just like to help you. I've worked in a restaurant before. I could chop things like she's doing."

Chop things like she's doing? I looked at Paula. She froze, her sharp chef's knife poised in mid-chop. I could tell from her expression that she was visualizing Marissa's head on her chopping block in place of the ham.

"Nobody but employees allowed in the kitchen," I said. "Department of Health rules. You and the boys help yourselves to more coffee, and I'll call and check on the status of that awful yellow tape around Rick's house just as soon as I get a chance."

She smiled. "If you're sure…"

"I'm sure."

She turned to leave, and I heard the bell over the front door jingle, signaling someone leaving or arriving.

"I'll get it," I said, setting down my cocoa and following Marissa out front.

Bryan Kollar beamed from across the room. Great. He and Marissa could have a phony smile contest.

"Brought those papers by." He held out a large brown envelope.

I recalled quite distinctly telling him during our phone conversation of the night before that I didn't want him to do that. However, suddenly I saw a way to get rid of two annoying pests with one swat.

"Bryan, this is Marissa Malone, Rick's mother." Let them bug each other and leave me out of the loop. "She's probably the one you need to talk to about buying that piece of property from Rick's estate. She's probably going to inherit it, not me."

He turned on a dime and focused all his charm on her. She radiated that charm right back. We were into severe charm overload, and they'd only just met.

"Marissa," he said, slipping the envelope under his arm so he could take her hand between both of his. "I had no idea Rick's mother would be so beautiful. I'm delighted to meet you."

"Bryan Kollar," she said. "I've heard so much about you. I can't believe I'm actually meeting you in person."

"Let's sit down and talk."

Together they moved to a table on the far side of the room from the table where Brad and Clint lingered over their coffee, watching their mother intently. Studying the craft of being a con artist?

I took coffee to Marissa and Bryan. I'd like to say I did it to be polite, but I actually did it to be annoying. If Bryan thought my cookies were poison, he probably didn't indulge in caffeine, either. I just wanted to see how far he'd go in his efforts to lay a con job on Marissa.

When I came out to write the specials on the big chalk board, all four of them were gone. Bryan hadn't drunk his coffee. At least he was consistent in his dietary habits.

ॐॐ

After the lunch crowd had cleared out and Paula and I got the place cleaned up for the next day, I called Trent.

"How's the removal of that awful yellow tape going?" I asked. "Rick's place ready for his family members to have a big reunion? The sooner we get them out of my place, the sooner you and I can play games there." I thought I'd give him a little extra incentive to get rid of the crime scene tape.

"We've run into a little problem."

My heart sank. I did not want to hear about a problem, no matter how little. "What kind of a problem?"

"Did Rick have a girlfriend?"

"Probably. He usually did. Why? Do we have somebody else who wants to move in his place? There's a Motel Six just a few miles away."

Trent cleared his throat. "We need another day with the house."

"No!" A collage of images from the past twenty-four hours flashed through my mind...the boys snoring in my living room, Marissa hogging the bathroom, strange people staggering around everywhere. "I need possession of Rick's house much worse than you do!"

"Sorry. Not yet. Kick those people out. Send them to a motel."

"They're Rick's family!"

60

"Since when does that matter? You don't owe Rick's family anything."

"No, I don't owe them anything. I didn't mean that. I just mean they're like Rick. I'll do my best to send them to a motel, but they're very difficult to get rid of."

"Well, you're going to have to figure out something. We've found female remains in the wreckage of Rick's car. We need to identify who died in that car with him, so that means we're going to be spending more time in the house."

I flinched at that news. "Damn. Dating Rick is enough punishment for any woman. Really sucks that dating him got her killed. You have no idea who it is?"

"So far we haven't found anything in the house that would identify her. We're checking missing persons reports. I was hoping you might have some idea."

"I figured that was why he wanted the divorce all of a sudden, because he had somebody, but I have no idea who it was. Do you think she might be the reason he was killed? Maybe she was married and her husband killed both of them."

"That's possible."

"I'm glad I have an alibi so you can't think his estranged wife killed both of them."

"I'm glad too."

I was making a joke. Trent sounded way too serious.

We hung up and I returned my phone to my purse.

61

"Did you lock the front door yet?" Paula asked, coming up beside me.

"No, not yet. Getting ready to do that right now."

"Still have your guests tonight?"

"They're gone for the moment. Maybe they'll decide to get a motel with unlimited hot water." I crossed the room to the front door.

A small boy who looked as if he'd sprung straight out of the pages of a Dickens' novel looked through the glass at me with large, soulful brown eyes. A shock of dark hair fell over his forehead, completing the image. I resisted the urge to grab a handful of cookies and give them to him. Probably not a good idea. All those legal liabilities. I opened the door to tell him we were closed.

"Did you kill my daddy?" he asked.

Chapter Nine

Before I could get my jaw off the ground, a woman stepped up behind the boy. She was barely taller than he was and had the same large Bambi eyes though her features were sharp and her hair was bright red, a shade of red that Mother Nature was never going to claim. "Now, Rickie, don't be rude to Daddy's new wife."

Once again Paula came to my rescue. "Sorry, we're closed." She tried to shut the door, but the woman caught the edge and held it open.

"You must be Lindsay. I'm Grace Ganyon, and this is Rickie, Jr." She extended a small hand with inch long nails that matched her hair. They were similar to Marissa's, but Grace's polish was chipped. Out of habit I accepted her hand. Small but hard and tough. "Rick told us so much about you. He always said if anything happened to him, we could count on you to help us."

I was pretty sure Rick did not say any such thing. "Odd. He never mentioned you all."

Grace heaved a deep sigh. "Rick wasn't a real responsible dad."

That I could believe.

"Can I have a cookie?" the boy asked, shoving into the room and heading for the display case.

63

Rude, pushy…yeah, he could be Rick's son.

Which meant I probably had some sort of obligation to him since I was currently in charge of Rick's estate.

Damn.

"Might as well." I sighed and opened the door wider to allow Grace inside.

Paula shot me a disgusted look, locked the door behind Grace and flipped the sign to "Closed."

Nice gesture, but if there were more of Rick's relations out there, I doubted a simple sign would discourage them.

I got cookies and Cokes for the kid and his mom, and we sat down at a table.

Paula came over. "Where's your cell phone?"

"In my purse."

She waited silently while I got my purse, took out my phone and laid it on the table, then she nodded. "I've got to pick up Zach from daycare, but I'll have my phone with me. Call me if you need…anything."

"Got it," I said. I appreciated the offer but thought she might be overreacting a little. Grace and the kid were obnoxious and pushy, but I couldn't imagine I'd need help in dealing with them. Well, maybe to get them to go away.

Paula left through the kitchen.

"Thank you so much," Grace said. "We haven't had anything to eat since breakfast."

"Breakfast sucked." The boy talked around a mouthful of cookie.

Grace patted his grungy little hand and looked pitiful. "The motel we're staying at didn't have a very good free breakfast. Just some cereal and stale pastries."

"Well, bless your hearts," I said. Grace either didn't notice or chose to ignore my sarcastic tone. However, if this was Rick's son, I supposed the least I could do was feed him, something Rick had apparently never done. "I could make you a sandwich." Paula would have scowled at me if she'd been there to hear my offer.

Grace grabbed my hand. Lots of grabby folks from Crappie Creek. "Thank you! Rick said you were a nice person."

I rose, pulling my hand from her grasp. I couldn't take any more. It was one thing to tolerate a load of crappie from Rick's mother, but I wasn't sure this woman had ever been his wife or the mother of his son. "When did you last talk to Rick?" I asked.

She smiled wanly. "It's been a while."

I smiled smugly. "That explains it. If you'd talked to him recently, he wouldn't have told you I was nice."

I went back to the kitchen and slapped together a couple of sandwiches then took them out to Grace and Rickie, Jr. They dove into the food as if they were starving. Maybe they really were.

"I'm glad to hear you've got a motel room because the cops are keeping Rick's house for another day, and my guest room is full," I said in an effort to thwart any ideas they might have on that front.

Grace swallowed her bite of sandwich and took a slow sip of her drink. "Well, we weren't really planning to stay at the motel another night. Rick has never paid child support, and money's a little tight right now." Her face crinkled, and she looked as if she might be going to cry. Actually, that's not quite true. She looked as if she might be going to pretend to cry.

"Mama, do we have to sleep with the bugs again tonight?"

Melodrama. Another element that suggested this boy had Rick's DNA.

"No, baby, we'll sleep in the car tonight."

I sank down in the chair beside Grace, ready to launch my defense against the attack I knew was coming. "You don't want to come to my house. You'd have to take the basement, and I have a lot of bugs down there, mostly spiders. Big ones. So big they catch birds instead of flies in their webs."

"I could sleep on the sofa, and Rickie would be happy on the floor with just a blanket to wrap up in. It would be better than my car."

"Sorry, those spots are already taken. But you might persuade Rick's mom to let you share the guest bed."

I had a feeling that would get a reaction, and it did.

Grace no longer looked as if she was going to cry. Suddenly she looked as if she was going to bite. "Mary's staying at your house?"

I wasn't sure if Mary was a nickname for Marissa or vice versa, and I had no idea what name was on that woman's birth certificate, so I ignored the whole issue. "Rick's mother and his two brothers are staying at my house. I have a small house. We've already hit way beyond cozy."

"She's probably the one who killed Rick."

I arched a dubious eyebrow. "You think Marissa would kill her own son?"

"She sure wasn't much of a mother. Rick lived with his daddy most of the time."

"Where's Daddy now?" She might slip up and tell the truth.

Her dark eyes narrowed. "Why do you want to know?"

"I thought he might want to join the slumber party at my house."

She blinked a couple of times. In all those purported discussions between Rick and her about me, I guess he forgot to tell her how sarcastic I can be.

"I don't know," she mumbled and went back to eating her sandwich.

"So you think Rick's mother killed him because he liked his father best?"

She shrugged. "I wouldn't put anything past that woman. Rick was working on a big deal, and she wanted in, but he wouldn't let her. Made her pretty mad."

Apparently Rick actually had been in recent contact with his family. "What kind of a deal?"

"How would I know? Nobody ever tells me anything."

"I know just what you mean. Rick never told me he was married before." A happy thought crossed my mind. Maybe he'd never bothered to get a divorce. Maybe he and I had never been married.

"We were married in the eyes of God!" Grace protested.

My hope for that avenue of escape withered and died. "What about the eyes of the legal system?"

She cast a glance at Rickie, Jr., who had finished his sandwich and was starting on his second cookie. "Mary wouldn't stand for that," she mumbled.

Suddenly I felt sorry for this woman. Pregnant, alone and up against Marissa, then raising a son with no help from the worthless father. I told myself it wasn't my problem and I should just send them on their way with a dozen cookies in a to-go bag. I assured myself I had no responsibility for these people even though I had access to Rick's property and Rick might—emphasis on the *might*—have fathered this boy and failed to provide for him.

All my arguments with myself were pointless.

"You can stay at my place tonight," I said with a sigh of resignation. "I'll borrow an air mattress from my neighbor."

I blame my mother for imbuing me with an over-active sense of responsibility. Or maybe it was Rick's fault. He had so little that I learned to make up for his failings.

Grace teared up and grabbed my hand again. "Oh, thank you! Rick was right. You are a good person."

"We don't have to sleep with the bugs again tonight?" Rickie asked.

There was something about that kid that got on my nerves. He must belong to Rick. "No guarantees," I said. "I have a no-kill policy on all creatures at my house."

❧⚜

Grace and Rickie's car was an old, rusty Ford that rattled and spewed black smoke as they followed me home. I told myself I was doing the right thing even if I didn't especially like these people. Karma had done me a favor by getting Rick out of my life. I had to pass on the good deeds or Karma might get mad at me and throw Rick back.

"This is nice," Grace said as she and Rickie climbed my porch steps. Whether she meant it or not, at least she had better manners than Marissa.

Nah, she must mean it. I hadn't seen any sign of manners.

I opened the door and invited them in.

Henry, waiting just inside, gave them a once-over and decided to ignore them. He head-bumped my leg then trotted off toward the kitchen without making any move to attack them. One vote against Rickie being Rick's son.

"Have a seat, let me feed my cat, and I'll be right back. After I answer my cell phone." My cell phone had begun playing Hoyt Axton's *Wild Bull Rider*. Fred's ring tone. Not that he'd ever been a bull rider. Well, he could have for all I know, but he'd have made the bull take a shower first, so I doubted it. However, the song reflected his attitude.

I took my phone from my purse. "Hello." I followed Henry to the kitchen.

"Now who have you brought home?" he asked.

"Rick's son and the boy's mother." I filled Henry's bowl.

Fred was silent for a long moment. Got him again! "Are you sure?" he asked.

"Of course not."

"Those other people are gone?"

"I don't know. I haven't seen them in several hours, so I'm hoping they've moved on to bigger and better swindles." I closed the pantry door firmly so Henry couldn't get in and help himself to his cat food, something he'd done before, and told Fred about Bryan and Marissa. "Maybe they'll stay with him tonight."

"That would be good. I really don't trust those people. Last night one of the boys was outside your house, trying to peer inside the windows."

"What? Omigawd! When?" I shivered at the thought of somebody peering into my house. "And why?"

"Twelve minutes after midnight, and I have no idea why. I'm not psychic. I thought at first it was Rick since he's done that sort of thing more than once in the past. Then I realized it must be one of his brothers since he's dead. I went outside to confront him, but he was gone by the time I got there."

"Which brother was it?"

"I don't know. They look a lot alike, and it was dark. Which one was wearing black last night?"

I hadn't paid much attention to the boys, but I was pretty sure they had both been wearing faded jeans and light-colored T-shirts. "Neither one of them. Well, not before we went to bed, anyway. Maybe they had black pajamas. Damn! Peeking in the window? That's creepy! Are you sure it was one of them?"

"Do they have a fourth brother?"

"I hope not, but it's possible. Rick's relatives just keep coming out of the woodwork."

"I'll see what I can find out."

He hung up. If I needed an air mattress, I'd have to call him back.

But that turned out to be unnecessary. Marissa phoned to say she and the boys were going to dinner with Bryan and would all be staying at his three bedroom condo on the Plaza. I smiled as I disconnected the call. I could just see Marissa and Bryan sitting across the table from each other at dinner, both trying for the biggest smile. They'd light up the entire restaurant.

I strolled back into the living room to tell Grace and Rickie they would have a bed and a sofa and wouldn't have to sleep on the floor or in the basement with the giant spiders. Grace was sitting on the sofa, thumbing through my coffee table book of cats while Rickie sat on the floor enthusiastically pumping the treadle of my grandmother's antique Singer sewing machine.

"Stop that!"

Rickie continued as if he hadn't heard me.

Grace looked up. "He's just playing. He's not hurting anything."

"Actually, he is. That machine is over a hundred years old, but it used to work before your son got hold of it!"

"Rickie, don't do that."

He stopped and glared at me.

"You might want to ask my permission before you play with anything else," I said.

He shrugged. "You haven't got any of the good channels. Like I could see them anyway on that little television. What am I supposed to do?"

"I don't know. Go outside and play in the traffic."

Grace laughed. "That's funny! Go outside and play in the traffic!"

No sense of sarcasm. "Why don't you read a book? I have lots of books."

He snorted. "I'm a kid. I don't read books."

"Don't you have any toys with you?"

"Go out to the car and get one of your games," Grace said.

"If I do, can we have pizza for dinner?"

Pizza for the third night in a row? What was a little high cholesterol compared to getting that kid settled down for a few hours? "Yes! If you'll sit in a corner and not touch anything for the rest of the evening, I'll get you a pizza."

He took Grace's car keys and went out the door.

"He's had a rough life," Grace said, "what with not having a daddy." She sighed and looked sad.

"How old was he when Rick left?"

"Just a baby."

"What did he mean at the restaurant about me killing his daddy?"

She shrugged and laid the book back on the coffee table. "He blames you for taking his daddy away from us."

"Excuse me? Rick was already living in Kansas City when I met him!"

"He's a kid. He doesn't always understand grown up stuff."

I'd be willing to bet he understood whatever she told him. I found myself wishing for Mama and the boys as house guests instead of these two.

My cell phone rang, diverting me from thoughts of choking Grace.

Trent.

I answered the call and went into the kitchen for a little privacy.

"Do you still have house guests, or would you like a cop to keep you warm tonight?"

I groaned. "Marissa and the boys are spending the night with Bryan Kollar, but Grace and Rickie, Jr., are here."

He said a few ugly words.

"I agree. Just take down that damned crime scene tape, and maybe tomorrow you can be my house guest."

"Working on it," he said.

The front door slammed, and the sound of something breaking came from the living room. Rickie was back in the house.

"Have you had a vasectomy?" I asked Trent.

"What? No!"

"Maybe you should give it some thought."

Chapter Ten

Rickie and Grace were no happier about being rousted out of bed at four in the morning than Mama and the boys had been. That kid sure could whine. Not for the first time, I sent up a prayer of thanks that Rick and I had never had kids.

Of course they came to the restaurant for breakfast. Our featured special that morning was Chocolate Gravy served over hot biscuits drenched in butter. Rickie had four servings. He'd probably be on a sugar high for the rest of the day. But that was Grace's problem, not mine. I didn't force feed him those biscuits and chocolate gravy, and she didn't stop him from eating them.

On one of my trips through the room to serve customers, Grace waved me over to their table. "Rickie's getting restless. I'm going to take him to a park or something. We'll be back before you close."

I gave her a smile as phony as anything Bryan or Marissa could produce. "Have fun. Don't forget to write."

She blinked a couple of times then, unable to figure out what I meant, just nodded.

Trent called in the middle of the lunch rush. Normally I don't answer any calls during those hours. My friends know that, and they wait until after closing time. So when I heard Trent's ring tone, I knew it must be important. Balancing a tray of sandwiches and cookies in one hand, I pulled my phone from my pocket with the other. "Hello?"

"I just wanted to let you know we're taking down the crime scene tape from Rick's house today."

"Thank you!"

"Call me later."

I wanted to jump and shout and laugh and yell. Instead I shoved my phone back into my pocket and took the food out to the customers. There would be time to celebrate tonight. Just Trent and me. The thought put a big smile on my face that didn't disappear even when a customer left a quarter tip.

After Paula and I closed, I dashed home with the intention of putting my sheets in the washer immediately. I only have one set of sheets for each bed. That way I save on storage room, and I never have to try to fold that stupid fitted sheet.

Even the sight of two cars parked in front of my house, one a shiny Cadillac and the other a battered Ford, didn't diminish my happiness. All I had to do was send them to Rick's house and let them destroy the furniture and each other. I didn't care if they totally demolished everything, even the house itself.

All five of them burst from their cars and converged on me as soon as I started across the yard. I made a mad dash for the door but barely got the key in the lock before they hit the front porch.

"The tape's gone, and my boys and I need to get in!" Marissa shouted.

"Don't let her! She has no right to be there! That's my son's inheritance!" Grace shouted, though her high pitched voice was no competition for Marissa's powerful tones.

"Mama, I don't like that woman!" Rickie whined.

Brad and Clint remained silent, hanging around the fringes. One of them was a peeping Tom, but it could be worse. They could both be like Rickie.

I spun around to face them, my back against the door. "Go, all of you! There's five bedrooms. Sort it out on your own." I waved my hands in an outward gesture.

"It's locked!" Marissa said.

"We can't get in," Grace added.

Damn. Of course the door was locked, and I distinctly remembered throwing my key at Rick the night I moved out. Hit him on the nose. One of my better memories.

The cops got in. There had to be a way. I'd call Trent and ask him. If Rick's relatives couldn't get in, apparently the cops hadn't kicked down the door.

"Stay here," I said. "I'll make a phone call and get you in."

Marissa and Grace began shouting and grabbing at me. I got the door open and slid inside, closing it behind me, almost getting somebody's hand. For a moment I leaned against it, trying to catch my breath and calm down. Thank goodness Rick had never insisted on spending Thanksgiving with his family! I'd have had to kill somebody with the carving knife.

Outside Grace and Marissa were still shouting at each other and Rickie was still whining. The boys were still silent. Probably knew there was no point in trying to out-shout their mother.

Henry trotted up, meowing in a complaining voice.

"Don't worry," I assured him. "I'm not going to let them inside. But if they get in, you have my permission to attack. Just be careful of Marissa. I'm not sure she's had her rabies shots."

My cell phone rang. Fred. The moment I heard his ring tone, I realized I didn't have to call the cops or get a key. I had a neighbor who possessed all sorts of arcane knowledge about breaking and entering.

"I'm so glad you called," I said, following Henry to the kitchen while I talked. Priorities. Feeding my cat was even more important than getting rid of the rabid relatives. At least, that was Henry's opinion.

"Are you aware you have a screaming horde on your front porch?" Fred asked.

"I do recall seeing something like that, and I need you to help me get rid of them." I poured food into Henry's bowl.

"The machine gun again?"

"Only if you have bullets in it." Henry dove into his food with enthusiasm. It took so little to make him happy. Much better son than Rickie.

"I would really enjoy that, but I don't think it would be a good idea. Your buddy Trent would be upset. He's so narrow-minded about things like that."

"Some friend you are, won't even kill a few people for me. Fine, at least go with me to Rick's house and pick the lock so I can get them inside."

"That's actually what I called about."

"Really? You knew I didn't have a key?"

"I didn't know, but it doesn't surprise me. Threw it in Rick's face when you left, didn't you?"

Sometimes Fred scares me with how much he knows. Or guesses. "Hit him on the nose."

"Good for you. I'll get you in the house now that the crime scene tape's gone—"

"How did you know the tape's gone?" See what I mean about the things he knows?

"It's public information. I'll get you in, but we have to search that house before you let that barbarian horde in there to destroy evidence."

"What evidence? The cops have been all over that house the last few days. They won't have left anything." Henry finished the last morsel of food, looked up and asked politely to go outside. Grace should have got a cat instead of having a son.

"That's possible, but we need to look anyway," Fred said. "The police found pieces of a computer in the wreckage, but they didn't find a backup drive in the house or at his office."

"Maybe he didn't have one." I opened the back door and let Henry out.

"Maybe. But that's unlikely considering all the details he had to keep track of for his business. If anything had happened to his original files, he'd have had some real problems. I feel certain he left a backup somewhere. You need to sneak out your kitchen door then go down the alley, and I'll pick you up at the end of the block."

"What about the horde?"

"Be sure all your doors and windows are locked. If they get bad enough, maybe somebody will call the police and report them for disturbing the peace." He hung up.

I looked at my inert cell phone. Rick's relatives were strange, no doubt about it, but my friend was a little strange too.

Nevertheless, I headed out the back door, locking up carefully behind myself. At least I'd get to ride in Fred's 1968 vintage white Mercedes. He was very picky about that car and would probably complain later about finding long red hairs everywhere. Like I pulled them out and dropped them on purpose.

Okay, maybe a couple just to annoy him.

I skulked across my back yard and through the bushes. Henry was lying on his stomach in the weeds, watching some creature intently. He gave me a quick, frowning look when I stepped on a stick and made a noise, then went back to studying his invisible prey. Sometimes I wondered if he had hallucinations, but I never brought it up.

Fred was waiting when I got to the end of the alley. I slid in, sank onto the soft leather seat, and we drove away, going exactly the speed limit, not one mile over. That was enough to drive me crazy. I consider speed limits to be suggestions for people who don't drive very well. Those people annoy me when they get in my way. And just for the record, Trent has steadfastly refused to fix even one speeding ticket for me. We've had a few discussions about that and will, I'm sure, have a few more.

"There's no evidence Rickie is Rick's son," Fred said as he eased around a corner. "The father on his birth certificate is listed as *unknown*."

"That's interesting. So all that prattle about Rick deserting her and his son was just BS?"

"I said there's no evidence that Rickie is Rick's son. I didn't say there was any evidence he isn't. Grace could have put unknown father on the birth certificate so she'd be eligible for government assistance for the boy. She's getting a check for him every month. That would be a scam Rick would come up with."

I sighed. "Yes, it's exactly something he would come up with. Find any evidence they were married or living together?"

"No marriage certificate on file. You were Rick's only wife."

"Damn."

He turned onto Rick's street, and I cringed, looking around for bits and pieces of Rick even though I knew the cops had taken away all the evidence of the explosion. Still, it was creepy.

"By the way, Grace Ganyon isn't her real name," Fred said.

"What a surprise. What is it?"

"Gail Haskell."

I shook my head as we pulled into the driveway. "What about Marissa?"

"Mary Kramer."

"And the boys?"

"Daniel Ray Kramer and Michael Lee Kramer."

"Which is which?"

"Who knows?" Fred set the parking brake.

"I'm afraid to ask what Rick's real name is."

"It's actually Richard Wayne Kramer."

"Astonishing. That's the first thing I know of that Rick didn't lie about."

I shuddered as I got out of the car. I didn't see any pieces of Rick's SUV or of Rick, but the driveway was scorched black from the explosion. Just a few days ago Rick and some unknown woman had pulled out of the garage to the very spot where Fred's car was parked. They were going somewhere, preparing to move on with their lives. Maybe Rick was even thinking about me when the blast hit, considering the fact that he was on his way to sign our divorce papers.

Nah. He was probably thinking about the woman who got blown to bits or maybe about whatever he was planning to do with the property he bought from Bryan Kollar's parents.

Fred and I walked across the porch and up to the ornate front door, oak with beveled glass panes. I remembered when Rick and I were building the house and picked out that door. Well, actually, he picked it out and I said okay.

Fred bent over the lock, did some magic, and the door opened.

We entered and Fred locked the door behind us.

The house had a faintly chemical odor, probably from something the cops did. I looked around at the room and the furniture that had once been familiar.

No wonder Trent never complained about my relaxed style of housekeeping. Cops were slobs. Fingerprint powder dusted most of the furniture, and they'd left footprints on the champagne beige carpet. In the kitchen was more of the fingerprint powder as well as open drawers with the contents spilling out and dishes on the counter. Pigs.

"You search down here, and I'll take the bedrooms upstairs." Fred turned and started to leave.

"Wait! What am I looking for?"

"CDs, an external hard drive, a flash drive, a memory stick." I must have looked blank because he continued, "If you don't know what something is, set it out for me to look at."

"Got it."

I was glad I didn't have to go through the bedrooms. That would bring up some really unpleasant memories. Just being in the house was bad enough. It stole the sense of security and comfort I'd wrapped around myself the last couple of years and made me feel alone and unsure, the way I'd felt when I was married to Rickhead and we'd lived in the house.

When we'd moved in, I'd been excited about the large, spacious kitchen, a place to create my chocolate desserts. However, I'd opened Death by Chocolate shortly afterward so I really never did much cooking in the kitchen. I wondered briefly if Muffy or Becky or any of the others had used my former kitchen. They used my former husband so why shouldn't they use my former kitchen? Kind of a package deal.

I set about snooping through all the drawers and cabinets.

Half an hour and several hundred kitchen utensils later Fred strolled into the room holding a hair brush in one hand and a red plastic rectangle about an inch long in the other. "I think I found it."

"A used hair brush? That's disgusting! As ultra-fastidious as you are, I can't believe you're taking one of Rick's brushes."

Fred gave me a disdainful look and lifted the brush. "This is a sample of Rick's DNA." He held up the red rectangle. "And this is a flash drive which we hope holds backup files for Rick's computer."

"That little thing?"

"Eight gigabytes."

"Is that a lot?"

"Enough for data file backup."

"Where did you find it? How did the cops overlook it?"

Fred smiled. "In his own childish way, Rick was actually pretty clever. He hid it in plain sight in a bowl of those rectangular cinnamon candies. A good thing none of the cops had a sweet tooth."

"Well, let's get home and tell the rude relations they're set to move in. We can leave the door unlocked. Who cares if somebody breaks in and steals something?"

Fred glanced over his shoulder toward the living room. "Actually, that won't be necessary. When I came down the stairs, I saw Marissa's Cadillac approaching the house. They're probably on the porch by now."

"Damn. Since your car's in the driveway, I guess we can't sneak out the back door this time."

"I believe our best option is to open the front door and make a run for the car. If anybody grabs you, scream loudly."

"Got it. On the count of three…"

We made it past the screaming, grasping relations. "Enjoy!" I shouted, dodging Marissa's hand.

We got in Fred's car and crept slowly away. They could have caught us if they'd chased us, but they didn't. They didn't want us, just the house. When I looked back, the porch was empty. They were all inside destroying Rick's precious possessions. I smiled.

"You could drive a little faster," I said, eager to get home, put my sheets in the laundry and call Trent to plan an evening of fun and frivolity. "Aren't you excited about getting home to check out this backup thing?"

"Of course I am." Fred sounded as excited as I've ever heard him, which is about 1.5 on the excitement scale.

"Then live dangerously and go five miles over the speed limit."

"No," Fred replied.

I let out a loud sigh and settled in for the thirty minute ride.

Finally I was home alone with Henry who was waiting on the front porch. "Come in and have some catnip," I invited. "You're entitled after the last two nights."

I stripped my bed and put the sheets in the washer then called Trent. Of course he didn't answer. I left a message and gave Henry a saucer holding his drug of choice. He gave me a Cheshire cat grin of gratitude then turned his attention to the catnip.

He took a few dainty snorts then, unable to restrain himself, began licking and nibbling. Finally he put his face in the saucer and rolled in the remnants. He looked up, gave me another grin, this time with his big blue eyes slightly crossed, and lay down beside the saucer, purring loudly and happily.

My sheets were clean and dry and on my bed, and I was getting a little concerned when Trent finally called me back.

"I'm all alone except for Henry who's drunk and passed out," I said, trying to sound sexy, though that's a little difficult when discussing a drunk cat. "Got clean sheets on my bed and all I need for a perfect evening is a cop to share that bed."

"I'm sorry." He didn't sound at all sexy. "I've got to work late."

"How late?" I had a sinking feeling I would be going to bed alone again, a retroactive virgin for another night, maybe for the rest of my life.

"Very late. We think we've found the identity of the woman who died in the explosion with Rick, but we've got to be certain before we do anything. She's married to somebody big."

Chapter Eleven

There are certain disadvantages to owning a business that's open to the public. The biggest one is that anybody who wants to can stroll in and sit down.

I was cleaning up in the kitchen after lunch when Paula returned from the main room with a big tray of dirty dishes and a scowl. "Don't go out there," she said. "Go out the back door, and I'll tell them you left for Spain this morning."

"Oh, no. Marissa or Grace?"

She set her tray down on the counter and looked disgusted. "Marissa, Grace and Rickie, Jr. Can't you hear them?"

I regularly tuned out the noise of customers, but when she said that I became immediately aware of the clamor.

"You need to get your skinny butt back to Crappie Creek!" Marissa's loud voice. "This is none of your business. You're not entitled to anything of Rick's! If my son had wanted you to inherit, he'd have married you."

"He would have if he wasn't scared of you!" Grace's nasal tones. "I'm not asking for anything for myself, just for Rick's son, your grandson!"

"That brat is neither my grandson nor is he Rick's son!"

"He may not be your grandson, but he is Rick's son!"

"What are you implying, you idiot bimbo?"

I wondered that myself. What she was implying, I mean, not whether she was an idiot bimbo. That part was clear and indisputable.

"I don't hear the kid," I said. "Does that mean you bound and gagged him or is he just sitting quietly in a corner destroying the building while his mother hones her bitch skills?"

Paula opened the dishwasher and began loading dishes. "You're close. I caught him trying to get into the dessert display case to help himself, so I gave him most of what we had left...about a dozen cookies, four brownies, a piece of chocolate pie and half a pan of fudge."

We both smiled.

"What a kind, generous gesture," I said. "He'll probably throw up on Rick's carpet tonight."

"And he'll be on a sugar high and drive everybody crazy for the rest of the day."

The thought of Rickie with his normal obnoxious behavior accented by all that sugar was an awesome image.

I considered Paula's offer for me to leave, actually cast a longing look at the back door. I had no doubt Paula would be able to handle those people, but I couldn't do that to her. I wiped down the counter and sighed. "I'll go see what they want this time. They have a place to stay, and I saw plenty of frozen dinners in the refrigerator. What else could they want?"

"I think they're fighting over that piece of property Rick bought from Bryan Kollar's parents."

I frowned. "Really? The old flour mill that's been in his family for generations, blah, blah, blah? Something's definitely going on with that property. Maybe they've discovered oil in the parking lot."

I took my cell phone out of my pocket and called Fred, my own personal Google.

"Did you have fun last night playing with Rick's computer backup files?" I asked as soon as he answered.

"Yes, I did. I think I know why Rick was suddenly eager to sign those divorce papers."

"Does it have something to do with the Kollar flour mill?"

Fred was silent for a moment. "You're getting pretty good at this. How did you find out?"

"Marissa and Grace are sitting out front in Death by Chocolate, fighting about it."

"Those people are kind of like a fungus that grows on you, and you can't get rid of it, not even with two tons of Gold Bond Powder."

"The Fungus Folks. Very appropriate. So what was Rick planning to do with the flour mill that involved making a lot of money?"

"About a month ago he started buying up all the property in the area. From the documents on that flash drive, it looks like he's planning to build a shopping center."

"Really? Isn't that kind of out in the middle of nowhere?"

"So was the Plaza at one time."

"You think Rick had advance information that the area's going to be hot?"

"Probably, but I don't have enough data to speculate at this point."

"I know, just the facts. But you do have enough data to speculate that he wanted to be divorced from me before he finalized this big deal, right?"

"We'll never be able to prove it, of course, but that does appear to be the case. He was planning to make a lot of money and didn't want to share it with you."

"That's our Rick."

"He's been conducting all this business using a separate bank account he set up right after the two of you split."

"What?" A familiar anger I thought had gone away with Rick's death rose up again. "The SOB had a bank account where he's been stashing money so I couldn't find it? That so ticks me off! I have never made any effort to take his money. He's known all along what I want. I've never even asked for an accounting of what he owns! If he wasn't already dead, I'd kill that worthless, suspicious, conniving rat!"

"We tend to judge others' morals by our own standards. Rick can't be trusted, so he thought you couldn't be trusted either."

"Fine, whatever. He's dead now so I can't even yell at him." I certainly did not wish Rick undead, but I would have liked to tell him what I thought of him just one more time. I guess it's true, when people die you always think of things you wish you'd said to them. "Grace and Marissa can fight over the properties and that bank account. I want nothing to do with any of it."

"There's more. Supposedly Rick withdrew fifty thousand dollars from that bank account the afternoon of the day he was killed, roughly two hours after the time of his death."

The implications of that hit me like a punch to the gut. I'd have sat down if there'd been any place to sit. Instead, I leaned against the counter and tried to come up with an answer other than the obvious one. "What are you saying? How is that possible? Someone withdrew money after Rick was killed? Are you saying Rick's not dead?"

He heaved a sigh at my ignorance. "I said supposedly he withdrew the money. My guess is that it was somebody who looks like Rick and had access to Rick's personal information."

"Clint or Brad."

"When I saw one of them outside your window in the middle of the night, I thought for a minute it was Rick," he reminded me.

"That would mean they knew he was dead as soon as he was dead, a day before they supposedly got to town."

"Exactly."

I had to sit down then even if it was on the floor. "Grace said Marissa might have killed Rick because she wanted in on a deal he was working and he told her no." Marissa was beginning to make my mother look like Mother of the Year.

Like an evil creature conjured up by my dark thoughts, Marissa burst through the kitchen door. "Lindsay, I need—why are you sitting on the floor?"

I scrambled to my feet. "What? What do you need, *Marissa*?" I emphasized the name so Fred would know I was confronted by a possible murderer and might need rescuing.

Paula came up behind me. "You know you're not supposed to be in the kitchen, Marissa," she said firmly. Had she overheard enough of my conversation with Fred to know she might be taunting Rick's murderer?

Marissa rolled her eyes. "How am I going to talk to Lindsay if she never comes out of the kitchen and I can't come in here?"

"What do you want?" Paula demanded, her voice cold. All things considered, I'd rather face a murderous Marissa than mess with Paula, all five feet, two inches of her.

"I want to know what my son had in mind for that piece of property Bryan Kollar is so hot to get back," she said, her voice losing its phony graciousness and becoming as cold and hard as Paula's.

"I think you already know," I said, joining the cold, hard voice club. "You wanted in on the deal, but Rick refused."

Her eyes narrowed and became blue ice. "Why do you have your hand pressed to your head? Are you on your cell phone?"

"Yes."

"Who are you talking to?"

"My boyfriend, Trent, the cop." I figured *my boyfriend the cop* would sound more threatening to her than *my neighbor the nerd* since she hadn't seen Fred in action.

"Don't you think it's a little rude to be on your cell phone when you're having a conversation with a real person?"

"Hey, you interrupted my phone call, not vice versa!"

She shrugged and again became Miss Congeniality. "I'm meeting Bryan on the property in half an hour. I just wanted to know what the situation was before we began the bargaining process."

"You don't have anything to bargain with," Grace said from behind Marissa. It was a big kitchen, but it was getting crowded really fast. "I'm going out there too, and I'm going to tell Bryan that's my son's property, not yours."

Marissa whirled on her. "You need to stay out of this. You're way out of your league, and you're going to regret it if you don't back off."

I froze. Had Marissa just threatened to kill Grace? Not that she'd kill her in person, of course, but she had two underlings. "Where are Clint and Brad?"

Marissa glared at me for a moment as if trying to discern my thoughts. "Why do you want to know?"

Oh, just wondering if they're hiding out at the flour mill, getting ready to blow up Grace's car, or maybe still at home planting a bomb under her bed. "No reason," I said. "Just wondered why they weren't with you today."

"They're grown men. I don't keep track of them." She whirled and stormed out of the kitchen with Grace right behind her. Both were shouting.

"I'll meet you there," Fred said.

92

"Yeah, I suppose we need to be there to keep Marissa from killing Grace."

"That too, but mostly we need to find out what's going on. I'm curious about this flour mill that everybody wants."

"Really? You want to go to a deserted flour mill to meet with a bunch of psychos out of curiosity?"

"I'm leaving in five minutes." He gave me an address and hung up.

"You're not going out there with those crazy people, are you?" Paula asked.

"Fred's going to be there."

She shook her head. "I really don't think either one of you should go."

"I have to." I told her about Rick's hidden bank account, his purchase of all the properties in the vicinity of the flour mill and his plans to build a shopping center.

"I knew there had to be money or a woman involved for him to finally agree to your divorce," she said. "Or both."

I'd already told her what Trent had said the night before about Rick's latest and last girlfriend being married to somebody big.

"If only he'd died a couple of hours later, we could have been divorced and none of this would matter."

"But you weren't, and it does. Be careful. I don't trust Rick or any of his family and certainly not that creepy Bryan Kollar."

"Who knew Rick could cause as many problems dead as when he was alive?"

On my way out the door I grabbed a couple of Cookie Dough Cheesecake Bars. If Bryan Kollar gave me any grief, I could always hold them up in the form of a cross. With his aversion to chocolate and sugar, that should keep him at bay. As for Rick's rude relations, I wasn't sure anything could stop them, not even holy water.

Chapter Twelve

The Kollar Flour Mill was north of Kansas City in a desolate area not far from the banks of the Missouri River. In the early years of the twentieth century, it was probably a booming region, but that was a hundred years ago when the river was the major transportation route. Now we had a system of highways, none close. To get to the place, I had to travel several miles along a rutted dirt road, passing a couple of other crumbling buildings surrounded by trees and brush. I supposed those were also properties owned by Rick's estate, but nobody was trying to get them back.

The old mill was surrounded by a relatively clear area, *relatively* being the key word. Weeds grew thick and healthy, but only a few scrubby trees thrust up amongst the weeds as opposed to the large trees and dense brush in the rest of the area. I wondered briefly if enough flour had escaped from the mill to retard the growth of vegetation in the immediate area.

Nah, that didn't seem likely considering what a beneficial effect flour had on my desserts.

I parked in the weeds next to Marissa and Grace's cars. Too bad they'd got there before me. I'd have liked to see them tripping through the weeds in their four-inch heels. Neither Bryan nor Fred had arrived. No surprise that Fred hadn't. As slow as he drove, the meeting could be over and all of us home in bed before he got there.

I had no desire to hurry inside and listen to Marissa and Grace hurl insults at each other, so I sat in my car listening to country music and waiting for somebody else to arrive. Prior to meeting those two women, I would have said there's nothing like a good cat fight for entertainment, but the reality did not live up to the hype.

As I looked around the place, I had a hard time visualizing a shopping center with hundreds of people dashing from store to store. The only creatures dashing around at that moment were probably mice and spiders. Maybe a few snakes. What did Rick know that made him think this area could be renovated and profitable, so profitable he wanted to be sure I didn't stand a chance of getting part of those profits?

A few minutes later Bryan pulled up in a Jeep. He got out wearing jeans and sturdy boots. He'd been to the place before, knew what to expect.

I was torn between going in with Bryan or waiting for Fred to get there so I could see how freaked out he would be about the dust that was going to settle on his pristine car and all the weeds that would be touching it. I finally decided to go in with Bryan. I didn't want to miss the hoopla that was bound to occur when he met Grace and she pressed her claim. I slid out of my car and moved up beside him.

"Lindsay, I didn't expect to see you here." He gave me his television commercial smile though he looked confused.

"I wouldn't want to miss it." I gave him a bared-to-the-molars smile. I didn't want to tell him anything and ruin the surprise, so I just kept walking toward the building.

The door hung open, dangling on one rusted hinge, and I could hear Marissa and Grace sniping at each other even before I saw them in the dim interior.

"Ladies," I shouted, "Bryan's here!"

Marissa met him at the door and flung herself into his arms, giving him a passionate kiss. He returned her embrace.

Who's scamming who?

I walked inside and looked around the abandoned structure. It was a large building erected of rough timbers, several of which had rotted and fallen away leaving holes in the walls and ceiling. At the rear of the building a ladder with at least half the rungs broken led to the remnants of a storage area upstairs. Spider webs decorated the walls and ceiling, and a barn swallow darted about in the rafters. It wouldn't surprise me if what was left of the roof collapsed at any moment.

Other than dust and leaves, the building was empty. I'd expected remnants of antique equipment, but that had probably been sold off or stolen a long time ago.

Rickie stood in the far corner kicking the wall, gradually making one of the holes larger.

Bryan expected me to believe his parents wanted this place for sentimental reasons? Really?

If four scam artists—Rick, Bryan, Marissa and Grace—wanted it, there had to be money involved. A lot of money.

"Sweetheart," Bryan said, pulling away from Marissa but still holding her in his embrace, "I thought this was going to be a business meeting between you and me."

Grace strode over, cocked a hip and fisted her hand on it. "I hope you and this old woman weren't planning to talk business about my son's inheritance."

Bryan's smile remained in place even though he was obviously confused. "Who are you? Who is your son and what is he going to inherit?"

"I'm Grace Ganyon, and that boy over there is Rick's only child. He's going to inherit all his father's property, including this dump, so if you want to bargain about what happens to it, you need to talk to me, not her."

Marissa kept her arm firmly wrapped around Bryan's neck. "Pay no attention to that silly woman. She's been trying to pass that boy off as Rick's for years, but nobody believes her."

Bryan's gaze shifted from Marissa to Grace to Rickie then to me. "Is that Rick's son?"

I shrugged. "I have no idea. We're going to get a DNA test and find out."

"What?" Grace shrieked, stomping over to get in my face. "You want to make Rick's son take some kind of painful test?"

"It's not painful, and we won't know if we're testing Rick's son until the results come back."

She became the sad, pitiful mother again. "Poor Rickie. All his life he's had to deal with his father not claiming him, and now you want to put him through this."

I looked to the corner where Rickie had ceased kicking the wall and was carving something in the wood with a broken piece of glass. Poor Rickie.

"He'd have been worse off if Rick had claimed him," I assured her.

Bryan looked completely confused. Couldn't blame the man. He'd had no idea there was going to be a party.

"Good afternoon."

I turned at the sound of the familiar voice. Fred stood in the open doorway wearing a dark suit and conservative tie. "Fred Sommers," he said, extending a hand to Bryan.

Kollar blinked a couple of times, released Marissa and shook Fred's hand though without his usual enthusiasm. His perpetual smile had faded. "Bryan Kollar." He dropped Fred's hand and turned to Marissa. "What's going on? You insisted on seeing the property before you'd make a deal, but you didn't say anything about bringing all these people."

"I didn't bring them," Marissa protested. Despite her best efforts to look beautiful, self-possessed and unfazed, her jaw was clenched and her pouty lips scrunched into a thin line.

"I'm here on Ms. Powell's behalf." Fred moved past the lovers and came to stand beside me. "Information has recently come to my attention that this property in which we are currently situated was purchased by the deceased from monies that were community property though such funds were secreted from my client in an attempt to conceal such real property from his legal spouse, Ms. Powell."

I suppressed a laugh, but Bryan, Marissa and Grace stared at Fred in bewilderment tinged with a slight awe. I had to give him credit. He is good at the baffle them with bullshit thing. Only Rickie, over in the corner torturing a spider, was unimpressed. The evidence was building that he could be Rick's son.

Grace gaped at Fred. "No. That's...that's not right...what are you saying?"

"I thought..." Bryan gave a weak wave in Marissa's direction then looked at Grace. "But she said that kid..."

"If you intend to regain possession of the property in question in order to negotiate a larger profit margin upon completion of the shopping mall project, Mr. Kollar, that may not be an option since Rick owns the other properties around here and you could be subject to eminent domain." Not exactly a lie since he said *could* instead of *will*. I could probably hone my lying skills by listening to Fred.

Bryan's eyes were glazed. "What? Shopping mall? What shopping mall?"

Fred looked smug as if he'd just conned a piece of information out of Bryan. Of course, Fred usually looked smug so it was hard to be sure. "Are you saying you're not trying to get this property back so you can sell it for a larger profit when the shopping mall goes in here, Mr. Kollar?"

Bryan turned pale beneath his perfect tan. "Shopping mall? Here?"

Marissa smiled benignly, dollar signs appearing in her eyes. "Shopping mall. So that's what Rick was up to. That's what his big deal was."

Grace's jaw dropped, but then she recovered herself. "A whole shopping center?" A wide smile spread across her face. "A whole shopping center for my son."

"No," Bryan said, visibly attempting to recover his composure. "This place has been in my family for generations. Nobody's tearing it down to build a shopping center."

Fred folded his arms and looked extremely official. "That's out of your hands, Mr. Kollar. You no longer own the property."

Bryan Kollar, Mr. Body Beautiful with the seductive voice and perennial smile who charmed the entire city, men and women alike, was losing his cool. The famous sculptured jawline clenched. His gaze slid around the room from Fred to Marissa then to Grace, Rickie, me and back to Fred. "My family owns this place. Rick Kramer scammed my parents out of it, and I want it back."

Marissa stepped up and took his arm. "This is all a silly little legal technicality. Let's go somewhere alone." She glared at Grace and me. "Between the two of us, we can sort this out."

Bryan let her lead him toward the entrance.

Grace turned to her son. "Rickie, say good-bye to the nice man."

Rickie dropped his stick and ran toward Bryan Kollar, grabbing his leg before he could get out of the way. "Did you kill my daddy?"

Kid had a limited repertoire of accusations.

Bryan stood rooted to the spot, looking down at the psycho kid in astonishment. I knew exactly how he felt.

Marissa pried the kid's fingers loose, tugged on Bryan's arm, and the two of them headed out the door.

"Are we finished here?" I asked Fred. "Can we leave now?"

"You can. I want to look around."

Rickie charged over to Fred and grabbed his arm. "Did you kill my daddy?"

Fred looked down at him and Rickie stepped back. Nobody is impervious to Fred's glare. "No, but I thought about it," he said. "Would you like a piece of bubble gum?" Fred produced a colorful paper-wrapped object from his jacket pocket and presented it to Rickie.

The boy grabbed it, ripped off the paper and began to chew.

"What do you say to the nice man?" Grace prompted.

Rickie scrunched up his face and spit out the gum. "That sucks," he said.

I wasn't sure if Grace had meant for him to say *thank you* or if *that sucks* was another of the cute little phrases she'd taught the boy.

Grace glared at Fred then turned to her son. "Let's go." They hurried out of the building.

"That went well," I said sarcastically.

"Actually, it did. We found out Bryan Kollar didn't know about the shopping mall venture, but there's something here that's worth a lot of money to him."

I looked around the ramshackle structure. "Just offhand, I'd say it's not the building itself."

"Maybe. Maybe not." He produced a plastic bag, leaned down and picked up the wad of chewing gum Rickie had spit out.

"I do not believe you're picking up a piece of gum off this filthy floor. Please tell me you're not planning to clean the entire place before we leave. I'm not sweeping."

Fred put the bag containing the gum into his jacket pocket.

I gaped at him in amazement. "I'm hallucinating. The man who wears rubber gloves to take a shower did not just put a used piece of gum in his pocket."

"How did you know about the gloves?" He was teasing me. I'm pretty sure of it. "You could say I put a used piece of gum in my pocket, or you could say I just stored a sample of Rickie's DNA in my pocket."

Chapter Thirteen

I expected to get home a few minutes before Fred because I drive faster, but I had time to feed Henry, let him out, take a shower, make plans with Trent for the evening and mix up a fresh batch of cookie dough before Fred finally drove into his garage. I noticed that his car was once again clean and shiny. A car wash would explain some of the time lapse. I knew all that dust would freak him out.

I went to his house and knocked on his front door.

He opened the door and looked over my shoulder. "Are you alone?"

"Of course I'm alone. Why would you ask such a question?"

"You so rarely are these days."

I couldn't deny that. "For the moment, I'm alone."

"Come on in."

I entered Fred's house and went to sit on his pristine leather sofa. "The good news is, I think my career as the manager of a B&B is over. Rick's relations have his house to wreak havoc on. Trent's coming over later, and we expect to have a nice Friday night alone." I got a little thrill just thinking about our first night together.

Fred took off his jacket and settled into his recliner. "A word of advice, don't answer your door or your phone for anybody except me."

"Got it. And you don't call unless you're dying." After all this time and anticipation, I wasn't about to have the evening interrupted by anything less than a huge emergency.

"Not even if I have the results of Rickie's DNA test?"

I looked at him dubiously. "Can you get results that fast?"

He shrugged. "Probably not. But I told my friend to put a rush on it."

"You've already dropped that gum off?"

"Of course."

"With a friend?"

"Yes."

"You have another friend besides me?" I was only half-teasing. Fred never talks about his past, and nobody ever comes to visit him except Paula and me. At least, nobody that I know of. He could have a secret tunnel leading to his house that only his best friends get to use.

Nah. I'm his best friend.

"I do have other friends," he said, "but none like you."

I wasn't sure how he meant that but decided to take it as confirmation of my status as his best friend. "So what do you think makes the old flour mill so important to Bryan Kollar if he didn't already know about the plans for a shopping center?"

"At the current time, I don't have the answer to that question."

"But you have some ideas," I prompted. I felt certain he had a whole list of possibilities.

He shook his head. "I don't have enough data to speculate."

"You could make a SWAG." Fred's SWAGs (Some Wild-Assed Guess) are usually more accurate than most people's well-researched opinions.

"I could, but I won't. I'm going to spend the evening gathering more data. Did you ever find out the name of Rick's girlfriend who was in the explosion with him?"

I sighed. "Trent's so close-mouthed about all that cop stuff. You could hack into the police computer and get the name."

"Honestly, Lindsay, some of the things you expect me to do just amaze me."

But he didn't say he wouldn't.

"I'm making some fresh cookies. Come on over and have a few. The massive quantities of sugar will keep you awake all night so you can find some answers."

"Thank you, but you and Trent should have the entire evening alone."

I rose from the sofa. "If you change your mind, we still have a few hours before the *alone* part becomes critical."

"Are you going to wear those clothes?"

I looked down at my best jeans and red shirt. "Not all night."

"The gray silk blouse and matching slacks your mother gave you for Christmas might be more appealing."

I'd shoved those clothes in the back of my closet and forgotten about them. How did Fred even know I had them?

X-ray vision.

"I'll think about it."

Fred's rarely wrong, so I dragged out the clothes my mother gave me and put them on. Then, while I was thinking about her, I phoned her just to be certain she didn't call during the evening and interrupt me while I was wearing…or not wearing…those clothes she gave me.

"Are you on that cell phone?" she asked immediately.

Damn. I forgot about caller ID. "Yes, but it's okay. You won't be getting any of those evil signals in your brain, just me, and my brain's already doomed."

"Please call me back on your real phone."

I sighed, disconnected and called her back from my landline.

"I'm so glad you called, sweetheart. I just heard the news about Julia Akin."

I searched my brain trying to place the name. Probably one of Mother's friends that I met once twenty years ago and was expected to remember for the rest of my life. I had no idea if the news was good or bad, whether Mother loved or hated Julia, if I should commiserate or celebrate. "I hadn't heard about Julia Akin," I said, trying to be as noncommittal as possible.

"Oh, Lindsay! I didn't realize you didn't know! I'll be right over. You don't need to be alone when you hear this."

I was supposed to know who Julia Akin was, and my mother was coming over to tell me about her and interrupt my evening with Trent. "No, Mother, don't do that. I'm not alone."

"Who's there with you?"

There were plenty of spiders in the basement and Henry would be back soon. "Trent's on his way." He might be, and certainly would be as soon as he got off work.

"Oh. Trent." My mother's voice dripped icicles. But she sighed and relented. "Very well. At least you won't be alone tonight."

"No, I won't. I'll be just fine. Look, I'm really sorry about Julia, but I need to run. That may be Trent's car coming down the street." *May be.* Odds were it wasn't, but that was a technicality.

"Sweetheart, I don't think you understand about Julia. We need to talk about her."

I sank down onto the sofa, prepared for a pretentious, verbose recitation of poor Julia's troubles. "Okay, let's talk."

"That's the woman who died in the explosion with Rick." Give my mother credit, she can be succinct and to the point when the occasion demands.

Though I had nothing against the late Julia Akin, I was delighted to get that news. It would give me something to throw up to Fred, that my mother had this information before he did. "I appreciate your concern, but it really doesn't bother me that Rick had another girlfriend."

A long moment of silence ensued.

"Do you know who Julia Akin was?"

"Rick's fifty-seventh girlfriend since we got married? That's just a wild guess. I didn't really keep track of the number."

My mother heaved a long-suffering sigh. It wasn't easy having me for a daughter. I could appreciate that. I wouldn't want to have me for a daughter. "She's Thomas Akin's wife."

"Married? Bummer. I hope they didn't have kids."

"They didn't. Lindsay, Thomas Akin is a very prominent man in the area. He's on the board of several organizations as well as chairman of the Missouri Roads and Highways Commission."

This was all starting to make sense. "Mother, where did you hear about this? It's not on the news yet, is it?"

"No, but it will be soon. Brent Hathaway told your father. He heard it from Sam Carruthers."

The news was making the rounds of the elite of Kansas City. My mother was suffering from shame by association. It was one thing when her daughter's estranged husband dated strippers and store clerks, but now he'd branched out into my mother's world.

Everyone would know.

"I'm sorry, Mother. Marrying Rick was a huge mistake, but I can't take it back, and I can't undo his misdeeds. He's dead. She's dead. It's a done deal."

"When the television reporters come to interview you, please be circumspect in what you say."

I thought Mother was probably being a little paranoid about the TV reporters, but I wasn't going to argue with her. "I can be circumspect. How about, *No comment*?"

"Yes, that would be best. Have you decided yet when the funeral will be? We need to get that over with as quickly and discreetly as possible."

"Oh, well, about that..." Maybe I should have let my mother come over or gone to her place. I could handle the news about Julia, but I wasn't sure my mother could handle everything I had to tell her. "The funeral's been sort of taken out of my hands. Rick's family has arrived."

She gasped. If she had not had impeccable manners, she would have interrupted me with an expression of her astonishment.

"I know, I told you I didn't think Rick had a family, that he was hatched from an egg in an experimental laboratory and the scientist who did it committed suicide from remorse. But it turns out he has a mother, two brothers, a former girlfriend and maybe a son."

A long moment of dead silence.

"Mom? Are you okay? Is Dad there? Do I need to come over? Do I need to call 911?"

"What sort of people are they?"

"Loud, pushy, demanding. You're not going to want to invite them to Thanksgiving dinner."

"Where are they right now?"

"In Rick's house, probably destroying everything." I smiled at that image.

My cell phone broke into *Wild Bull Rider*. Fred.

"I gotta go, Mom. I'll let you know when the funeral is."

I hung up and answered Fred's call.

"I found out the name of Rick's girlfriend," he said.

"Me too. Julia Akin." *Bazinga! I said it first!*

"I suppose it's common knowledge already. That was bound to happen."

"If it's not, it will be soon. My mom's bridge club will be spreading the news to the far corners of the earth."

"I didn't realize your mother played bridge."

Poor Fred. I'd just scooped him and now he thought there was something he didn't know about my mother.

"She doesn't play bridge. I was just making a point. The news is going the rounds in her circle of acquaintances."

"I see."

"Sorry. Didn't mean to steal your thunder. Well, actually, I did mean to." I couldn't repress a short giggle. It's so seldom I'm able to beat Fred at his own game.

"Does your mother's fictitious bridge club know about the new highway extension planned for the area out by Kollar's Flour Mill?"

I sat bolt upright on the sofa. "So that's why Rick was buying up that property and planning a shopping center! Somehow Julia found out through her husband and told Rick."

"It would appear. Short of finding a good medium, I don't suppose we'll ever know exactly what happened, but apparently something along those lines did."

"I wonder what this will mean with respect to all those properties he bought? Will Marissa or Rickie or whoever gets them have to give them back since Rick had inside information he didn't reveal?"

"No, of course not. Julia probably broke a few laws when she shared the information about the highway, but they can't prosecute her or Rick now."

"You think Bryan Kollar could have known about the highway even though he didn't know about Rick's plans for the shopping center?"

"It's possible, but I don't think so. I need to do some more research on him." He hung up.

I sat there on the sofa mulling over this new information until I heard a knock on the door.

Trent.

I got up to let him in. Henry darted in alongside him. I was glad my cat liked my boyfriend. I'd have hated to have to choose between them.

Trent smiled, the green in his eyes dancing. He held out a bouquet of brightly colored flowers.

"They're beautiful!" I was impressed. Rick always gave me roses, but I really like lots of different flowers of different colors.

"You're beautiful." He pulled me into his arms and gave me a long, slow, delicious kiss.

"Want to go upstairs?" I whispered.

He laughed. "How about we go to dinner first? We've waited this long. Let's do this right."

I nodded. "I guess I'm just being a little paranoid. It's like the universe is scheming to keep you out of my bedroom, and we need to take advantage of this opportunity."

"This opportunity will last all night. We're not going to open the door to anybody, not even the fire department."

"Deal."

I put the flowers in a vase, gave Henry some catnip, and Trent and I went to a steak place with real napkins and candles on the table. I spilled red wine on my gray silk blouse. Should have worn the red shirt.

When we got home, Trent parked his car in my driveway rather than on the street. We were settling in for the night. I smiled as we walked across the yard to my house, his arm around my waist. I'd been waiting for this night for a long time, waiting for my divorce to be final and, more recently, waiting for Rick's relatives to go away. I had to work the next day, but it was Saturday and we only served brunch on Saturday so I could sleep—or whatever—until six o'clock, an extra two hours.

We went inside. I locked the door behind us and put on the chain then stepped into Trent's arms. He has the most luscious lips. I could kiss him for an hour or so and planned to do just that.

"Upstairs," I whispered against those wonderful lips.

"Mmm hmm," he agreed, kissing the side of my neck, working his way down, sending tingles all through my body.

His cell phone rang.

"Don't answer it."

He sighed and stopped the wonderful things he'd been doing. "I have to. That's my work phone."

I got an eerie feeling that Rick from his vantage point on the other side was somehow still manipulating my life. I was being paranoid again.

I went to the kitchen to get a Coke while Trent took his call.

When I came back he was sitting on the sofa with his hands in his lap holding his phone between them, his head down.

"You have to leave, don't you?" *Please say no!*

He nodded and lifted his head to look at me. His eyes were dark. "They got an anonymous call at the station. Somebody says he knows who killed Rick and wants to meet with me tonight to tell me. The caller has some information we didn't release to the public, so this could be legitimate."

Chapter Fourteen

I was sleeping soundly on the sofa when Trent returned. He woke me with a kiss on the cheek. I sat up and rubbed my eyes. "Did you catch the killer?"

Trent sank down beside me, and I could tell by the disgust on his face what the answer was going to be. "The informant never showed up."

"Damn. That sucks. What time is it?"

"Two a.m."

"Two a.m.? It was nine thirty when you left here. Did you wait all that time for some creep who wouldn't even give you his name?"

Trent leaned back and heaved a long sigh. "Sort of. He kept calling and saying he'd been delayed, so Lawson and I kept waiting until it got ridiculous. Obviously he knows something or he wouldn't have known..." He glanced at me. "He wouldn't have had that information we withheld. But he was jacking us around tonight."

I wrapped an arm about him and laid my head on his shoulder. "Want to come up to bed?" I tried to make my words sound suggestive, but my yawn in the middle of the sentence probably blew that attempt.

He laughed softly and kissed the top of my head. "Not when you have to get up in four hours and you're already asleep."

"I'm awake."

"Then why are you snoring?"

I lifted my head and peered at him in the dim light. "I wasn't snoring. Was I?"

He laughed again. "Tomorrow night. You and I. All night long then sleep all day Sunday. That'll be better anyway." He stood, pulling me to my feet. "Lock the door behind me then go straight upstairs to bed."

"Okay." I didn't protest. To be honest, I wasn't feeling very sexy at that moment, just sleepy and angry at whoever had led Trent and Lawson on a wild goose chase by claiming to have information about Rick's murder.

My paranoia was justified. Even dead, Rick was managing to keep Trent and me out of the bedroom.

ॐ

For once my mother hadn't overreacted.

I was in the kitchen of Death by Chocolate taking out a fresh pan of brownies when Paula came back to tell me a reporter from one of the local stations wanted to talk to me.

I set the brownies on a cooling rack and uttered a few swear words.

"Want me to tell her you're not here?" Paula asked.

"No, I'll get rid of her."

It was just after 11:00. We'd only been open a few minutes, so there weren't a lot of customers in the room. That was good. Maybe I'd be able to get

116

rid of the reporter quickly and easily without anybody noticing.

I walked over to the blond woman standing at the counter. "I'm Lindsay Powell. Can I help you?"

The man sitting beside her rose and turned on his video camera. No, we weren't going to be able to do this quickly, easily or discreetly.

The woman smiled. "Lindsay, I'm Wendy Turner with channel 7. Could we chat for a few minutes?"

"I'm pretty busy right now."

She looked around the near-empty room. "When would be a good time?"

"If this is about my ex-husband, I have no comment."

She raised an eyebrow. "Ex? You and Richard Kramer were divorced when he was killed?"

"Well, no, but we are now. I mean, he's dead, so we're not married anymore. That's like the ultimate divorce."

"Were you aware he was dating Julia Akin?"

"Rick and I were separated. I didn't keep up with his social life." Damn! I was talking to a reporter! Mother wasn't going to be happy.

"Do you think Thomas Akin murdered his wife and your husband?"

"What?" I grabbed a glass, poured myself a Coke and drank half in one gulp. Sure, I'd joked about that scenario but it would be ironic if, after all his cheating, Rick really was killed by a jealous husband.

"You haven't heard that the police took Mr. Akin in for questioning this morning?"

"No. No comment." It was probably a little late for that. I chugged the rest of the Coke.

"Was Julia Akin the reason you filed for divorce from your husband?"

"This is a place of business. You need to leave."

The bell above the door jingled as another customer came in. I hurried over to take his order then ran back to the kitchen. When I returned with the man's food, the reporter and photographer were gone. Whew! Dodged that bullet without spilling too many of my guts.

A couple of hours later the place was packed. Paula and I were both darting around, dispensing sandwiches and chocolate.

I was behind the counter, selecting chocolate chip cookies for the party of four in the corner...one gluten free, one without nuts and two regular...when I heard a familiar voice and looked up to see Detective Lawson standing at the counter, scowling. He always scowled so that didn't mean anything. I was focused on keeping the cookies separate and just gave him a quick smile and a nod. "Be right with you."

I gave the right cookies to the right people (later confirmed because nobody went into anaphylactic shock) then came back to the counter.

"Hey, Lawson, good to see you," I said. "What can I get for you? I recommend the brownies. They're especially good today. I've had four already, just for purposes of quality control, of course."

"You need to come outside."

My heart stopped. When you're involved with a cop and another cop wants to talk privately, that's scary. "Is it Trent? Is he okay?"

"Trent's fine. He asked me to do this since you and he..." He shrugged, turned and walked to the door.

I caught Paula's eye across the room and indicated that I was going outside. She looked around at the crowded room and held her hands out questioningly.

I shrugged and followed Lawson outside. When a cop beckons, one must follow.

A police cruiser was parked in a "No Parking" spot in front of the restaurant. Lawson opened the back door and pulled out a tall man.

Brad.

Clint slid out right behind him.

They weren't smiling.

"What's going on? What are they doing here? Why were they in the back of a cop car?"

"Detective Morrison arrested them last night for prostitution."

I had met Alicia Morrison, an attractive lady who often went undercover. "Prostitution?" I looked at the boys in complete disgust. They ducked their heads and looked ashamed. But like Rick, I'm sure they were only ashamed they'd been caught, not that they'd committed the crime.

"When Trent came in this morning and found out what happened, he asked me to get them released into your custody since they're Rick's brothers."

"My custody?" My hand clutched my throat in horror. "Oh, no! Why didn't he release them to their mother's custody? I don't want them!"

"He tried to get them released to Marissa, but she's got too many arrests on her record."

Why did that not surprise me? "Then take them back to jail! Prostitution?" I glared at the boys. "You tried to hire prostitutes? Are you nuts?"

"We didn't try to hire anybody," Brad protested, lifting his gaze and looking totally unrepentant.

"That woman was just sitting there in the bar looking lonely," Clint said. "She acted like she liked us. She should have told us she was a cop." He glowered at Lawson. "That's entrapment."

Marissa drove up and got out of her Cadillac at the same time I spotted Wendy Turner and her cameraman in the gathering crowd. A news van from another station pulled up behind Marissa's car. Oh, goody. We were all going to be famous, and my mother was going to have to get her valium prescription refilled.

Marissa was mad. She stomped up to her sons and backhanded both of them. "What is the matter with you? What were you thinking?"

"Ma'am," Lawson said, stepping between her and the boys, "you can't hit them."

"Oh, yes, I can! I gave birth to these sorry excuses for men, and that gives me the right to discipline them when they do something stupid, and propositioning a cop is one of the stupidest things I can think of!"

"But, Mama," Clint whined, "we needed some money! She didn't tell us she was a cop!"

120

Something about that didn't sound quite right. *We needed some money?* How did they plan to pay for sex if they needed money?

"She looked like a regular woman, and she smiled at us!" Brad said. "You told us yesterday to go make some money."

Marissa stepped around Lawson, grabbed Brad's hair in one hand and Clint's in the other and started to drag them away. "Tried to sell yourselves to a cop?"

Tried to sell yourselves to a cop? Omigawd! The implications of her words hit me like a ton of unsweetened chocolate straight to the gut. They hadn't been soliciting Morrison for sex, they'd been trying to sell it to her! This just got better and better.

"The two of you don't have a brain between you!" Marissa berated the boys as they stumbled along behind her. "We're about to be rich and you put all that at risk."

Wendy moved in front of her just before she reached her car. "I'm Wendy Turner with Channel 7. I'd love to hear about how the officer entrapped your sons."

I expected Marissa to backhand the reporter, but of course that wasn't her style. She was, first and foremost, a con artist. She ordered her sons to get in the car, then turned and smiled for the camera. "Thank you so much for giving me the opportunity to clear my sons' names."

All attention was focused on Marissa, and for the briefest of moments I thought I might be able to escape from the debacle. I turned to go back into the restaurant, but a reporter from the other station stepped in front of me. "How do you feel about having your brothers-in-law released to your custody?"

"My—they're not—I mean—how did you find out?"

"Police report. Your life has been pretty hectic for the last twenty-four hours, learning about your husband's affair with Julia Akin, then her husband being questioned by the police, and now your murdered husband's brothers have been arrested for prostitution. How are you holding up?"

I tried to beat down the panic as I looked at the scene around me. Marissa was smiling and babbling and tossing her hair for the six o'clock news. All my customers in the restaurant were looking out the window, watching the entertainment. A crowd had gathered on the sidewalk. There was no way I was going to escape this with even a modicum of dignity.

You know what they say...when life hands you a lemon, make Lemon Chocolate Pie.

I straightened and looked directly into the camera. "As long as I have plenty of my wonderful chocolate creations, I'm holding up just fine." I waved a hand toward the sign for my restaurant, Death by Chocolate. Yes, my mother was going to be horrified, but that's pretty much a constant state for her.

"We're getting ready to close now," I said, "but we'll be open again on Monday, and I'm going to create a special chocolate dessert that will help the families and friends of both victims, Rick and Julia, cope with this terrible disaster."

I smiled, waved to the camera and pushed my way into Death by Chocolate.

Paula gave me a smile and a thumbs-up sign.

Chapter Fifteen

After the chaos of the day, I thought I'd go home, take a nap, have a relaxing bubble bath, and be all rested by the time Trent arrived for our special night which was absolutely going to happen this time.

However, *relax* really isn't a part of my vocabulary or my life.

I tidied up the house, helped Henry stalk a few creatures, made some fresh cookies and put a roast in the oven. I have a talent for making chocolate desserts, but beyond that, my culinary skills are decidedly limited. Nevertheless, putting a roast with potatoes and onions into the oven and taking it out a couple of hours later was something even I could handle. Since Trent and I had already had a wonderful dinner the night before, I thought we'd stay in tonight. And maybe I'd hide his cell phone.

Predictably my mother called. I lucked out. Either my plug for Death by Chocolate didn't make the news, or my mother didn't watch that channel. She was upset over the interview Marissa gave about the boys, of course, but I escaped her censure. I commiserated with her concerning Rick's horrible family and got off the phone before she had a chance to ask about my plans for the evening.

I was starting upstairs to have a quick shower when someone knocked on the door. Henry had been going up with me, but he stopped on the first step, back arched and hair standing on end, snarled, and bounded down to the front door.

Rick was dead, so the person on my porch must be a particularly obnoxious magazine salesman, a serial killer, or one of Rick's relatives.

I went back down and peeked out the peephole.

Give the cat a prize! It was Marissa.

I opened the door. "Not a good time. I'm really busy right now."

She started to push past me and come inside anyway, but she only made it halfway before Henry bared his teeth and hissed at her.

She backed off. "Could we sit outside and chat for a minute?"

"If I give you ten minutes of my time, will you leave?"

"Of course." She turned and headed for my porch swing. "I so appreciate your doing this. My life has become a nightmare with my son's death and my other two boys doing foolish things because they're so grief-stricken."

"Can the crap," I said. "Tell me what you want. You've got nine and a half minutes."

She sat in the swing, and her expression changed, lost its artificial glow. "Straight talk. I can handle that. The thing is, I'm broke."

I was not about to sit beside her in the swing, so I stood. Besides, it gave me the advantage of looking down on her. "I'm so sorry to hear that. I guess the real estate business isn't going so well."

She sighed. "It's this economy. Everybody's so careful with their money these days."

"That must make running scams very difficult."

She glared at me then eased into a sad smile. "A couple of months ago I asked Rick to borrow some money. He turned me down flat. Then I heard through the grapevine that he was working on a deal that would make him millions, so I asked if he'd let me in on the deal. Again he refused."

I folded my arms and nodded. "Rick's selfish like that. Didn't let me in on it either."

"But now he's dead and we can both soon be rich."

I sucked in a breath and tried to keep my face impassive. Again I remembered Grace's comment that Marissa could have murdered her own son. It would appear she had motive.

"I have no desire to profit from anything Rick was involved in, and you may not get anything if Rickie really is Rick's son."

Her eyes narrowed to malevolent slits. "I will see to it that horrible child never gets a penny of my son's estate."

"Did you just threaten Rickie's life?"

Her smile returned. "Certainly not. I meant I'll fight Grace in every court in the country if I have to."

"Really? If you're broke, where are you going to get the money to hire a lawyer?"

Her smile widened. "That's what I want to talk to you about. I need to hire a lawyer to represent my sons who did a very foolish thing last night, but you know how boys are."

126

"I'm very well acquainted with how the boys who happen to be your sons are. I was married to one of them."

"Yes, and you'll be getting quite a lot of money from his estate, so it would only be fair if you'd advance some of that money to your husband's mother."

"Sorry, can't do it. I don't have access to his money."

"Of course you do. You were his wife." She didn't stop smiling, but her expression became tight.

"His estranged wife. We had no joint accounts."

"But you have money in your own account, and that's still community property since you were married to my son when you earned that money. Rick would want you to help his mother."

Through the screen door I heard Henry give a low growl. Sometimes I think that cat understands English.

"Rick refused to help you. What makes you think he'd want me to?"

"Because you're a better person than Rick was." Her voice actually had the ring of sincerity for the first time since I'd met her. "He said you were the most genuinely kind person he'd ever met."

For just a moment I felt a blink of compassion toward Rick. But that moment passed. "In other words, you think I'm a gullible sucker, somebody you can easily scam. I think your ten minutes are up. Good-bye." I took a step toward the door.

Marissa stood and laid a hand on my arm. "No. He said he could become a better person if he had

127

you in his life. That's why we all stayed away, to give him a chance."

Either she'd lied before when she said they were estranged because of a *silly fight* or she was lying now. Probably she lied both times. "Well, he didn't make it. He was still a worthless, cheating con artist when he died. Look, I got you into Rick's house. You're living there for free, you're eating his food. That's it. That's all you get from me. Now, if you'll excuse me..." I shook off her hand.

Marissa snorted. "Yeah, I'm living in a house with Grace and that awful child of hers. You have no idea how miserable that is."

"Actually, I do. They stayed here one night. If we find out that's not Rick's son, I'll see to it they have to leave. But until we get the DNA results—"

"*Until?* You've already ordered DNA tests?" Her eyes glittered with something resembling genuine happiness. A malevolent sort of happiness but real nevertheless.

"Yes, I have."

"Good." She smiled and started off the porch but then turned back. "If you could advance me just a thousand dollars—"

"No."

"Five hundred."

"No. You need to leave. My boyfriend the cop will be here any minute."

She left with alacrity.

I didn't expect Trent for another hour or two, but that translated to sixty or a hundred and twenty minutes. It could qualify for *any minute*.

I went over to Fred's house.

He opened the door before I knocked. "I was going to call you, but I saw that woman on your porch."

I went in and sat down on his sofa. No point in asking how he'd seen Marissa through all that foliage around my house. He has x-ray vision. I'm sure of it. "She wanted money. I told her no."

"Good. I saw you on TV." He took a seat on his matching recliner.

"The promo for Death by Chocolate?"

"Yes. You articulated very nicely, but your hair was a mess."

"This morning when I did my hair, I wasn't planning to be on TV!"

He shrugged. "Doesn't matter. Your hair's usually a mess."

"My hair's curly, and Kansas City is humid. In what world is that my fault?"

"I didn't say it was your fault. I was just making an observation."

"Fine. Look, I didn't come over here to discuss my hair. I think Marissa might have murdered Rick."

He nodded. His hair was immaculate, of course. "Filicide. It's more common than you might think."

I told him what Marissa had said about her financial situation and Rick's refusals to help her.

"That gives us at least two viable murder suspects. Thomas Akin doesn't have an alibi for the time of the murder. He knew about Rick and Julia. He hired a private detective to follow them."

I didn't ask where Fred came by that bit of information.

129

"What about Bryan Kollar? He wanted his parents' property back from Rick. Maybe he wanted it bad enough to kill him. You said you were going to investigate him further."

Fred drummed his fingers on the arm of his chair as if frustrated. "I did, but I haven't found anything suspicious yet. He took up bodybuilding in college, bought a small gym and turned it into a major success. He's single, an eligible bachelor about town. In high school, he was the skinny kid who got sand kicked in his face, so this whole bodybuilder thing is a major triumph for him."

"From a skinny kid to Mr. Body Beautiful? What about steroids? Maybe he killed Rick in a 'roid rage."

"When you see that kind of physical development, steroids are always a possibility, but I haven't found any evidence. What I do find intriguing about Bryan Kollar is the lack of information available. He's a local celebrity, but everything out there is very superficial, as if somebody has made an effort to hide any significant details. But if they're there, I'll find them."

"Why don't we go visit the detective Akin hired?" I enjoy these little jaunts with Fred. They're always interesting, informative, and sometimes I get to dress up and indulge my frustrated desire to be an actress. "If he was following them closely enough, he might have seen the murderer."

Fred nodded approvingly. "Good idea. I'll look into setting that up."

"And maybe Bryan Kollar's most recent girlfriend or gym manager or…well, I don't know.

Somebody who knows him. I could be your protégé who's interested in becoming a female bodybuilder."

He gave me a skeptical, arched eyebrow look. "You'd have to lie about how much Coke and chocolate you imbibe."

"Hey, if I can pretend to be a stripper, I can pull off a bodybuilder." I rose. "Now that you've insulted me, I'm going to go home and shower and get ready for Trent. Tonight is definitely The Night."

"What happened last night? Why did he leave so early, come back so late and leave again?"

I told him about the bogus informant.

"I wonder what information he had that made the police believe him."

"No idea, but I'm sure you'll figure it out."

"More than likely."

I went home and found Henry snoozing in the kitchen. That was odd. He always came to the door to greet me. "Some watch cat you are!"

He opened his eyes and gave me a quick glance before settling down to sleep again. In that brief glance, I saw that his eyes were slightly crossed.

He was drunk! Somehow he'd gotten into the catnip! I looked around. The drawer where I kept the catnip was open, and the bag of catnip was on the floor, showing signs of bite and claw marks with the contents scattered about.

Henry was a pretty impressive cat, but I would never have believed he'd be able to open a drawer. Still, the evidence spoke for itself.

I cleaned up the mess and left him snoozing while I went upstairs to shower.

131

I reached inside the shower curtain that wrapped around my antique claw-foot tub and turned on the hot water.

A man in my shower began cursing.

Terror shot through me. Someone had broken into my house while I was at Fred's! I'd left the front door open since I was coming right back and my guard-cat was there. Someone came in and gave Henry catnip so he could prowl my house without interruption. Was this Rick's killer, returned to do away with me?

Heart pounding, I grabbed my metal hair dryer and yanked back the shower curtain.

The wet man screamed.

I screamed louder and whacked him with the hair dryer.

Chapter Sixteen

"Lindsay, it's me!"

I halted my hair dryer in the middle of my second swing. Confusion replaced my fear. "Rick?" It couldn't be his ghost. That first swing had hit a solid object.

He climbed out of the tub and reached back to turn off the shower. "First you scald me and then you give me a concussion!"

This could not be happening. I must be hallucinating. Maybe somebody sneaked something extra into my last batch of brownies when I wasn't looking. "You're dead! What does a little hot water and a concussion matter to a dead man?"

He grabbed a red towel from the rack and began wiping his hair. One of my best towels, and now I'd have to burn it. "Is there blood?" he asked, examining the towel.

"How can there be blood? Dead people don't bleed!" I was desperately trying to hang onto his death.

"I'm not dead!"

I tossed my dryer into the sink in disgust. "Damn! I might have known! What are you doing here? Why did you pretend to be dead?"

He looked down at his soaked clothes. "Why did you turn on the shower without looking inside?"

"Because I always turn on the shower without looking inside! Why did you hide in my bathtub?"

"You always shower in the mornings! I thought I'd be safe here until you went to sleep. Why were you going to shower in the evening?"

I threw my arms into the air. "I had no idea there was a ban on evening showers! Had I but known, I'd have just continued to stink for the rest of the night!"

"So you're worried about how you'll smell for the rest of the night? That cop's coming over, isn't he? That's why you were going to take an evening shower!"

"What difference does it make? You're dead and we're not married any longer!"

"I'm not, and we are!"

"Are you all right, Lindsay? I heard a scream."

I turned to see Fred standing in the bathroom doorway. "No, I'm not all right! Rick's not dead!"

"That explains the lack of male DNA at the scene of the explosion," he said calmly.

I glared at him. "At a time when I could use a little consolation, all you do is spout off about DNA!"

"So the cops know I'm not dead?" Rick asked, his voice suddenly subdued.

"They're not certain yet," Fred said, "but they're beginning to speculate."

"Damn!" Rick sank down onto the toilet and put his head in his hands.

"Why didn't you warn me he might not be dead?" I demanded of Fred.

134

"I didn't want to upset you unnecessarily. I kept hoping they'd find something."

Rick lifted his head. "You're ghouls, both of you!"

"Well, you're a...an undead, a zombie, maybe a vampire," I said. "That's about as ghoulish as it gets. What's going on? Why aren't you dead?"

"Julia pulled the car out of the garage while I went back inside to get my wallet. I came out just as everything blew up. Scared the beejezus out of me, I can tell you! But I was thinking fast. I threw my wallet out into the rubble so they'd think I was dead, then I went inside, ran out the back door and kept running."

"To the condo you own in Prairie Village?" Fred asked.

"The condo he owns in Prairie Village?" I repeated. Prairie Village is an upscale suburb on the Kansas side. That condo probably cost at least twice what my little house cost. "What condo is that?"

Fred frowned. "Did I forget to tell you about the condo? Sorry. I just found it last night. I was going to tell you today, but then we got off on Marissa and Bryan."

Rick shot up from the toilet seat. "Marissa and Bryan?"

I shoved him back down. "A bank account and now a condo? How many more assets were you hiding from me? I told you I didn't want any of your stuff, so why were you going to all the trouble to hide it? Do you think I'm as despicable as you are? Is it true what Fred told me, that you judge everybody by your own immoral code?"

135

"Do you think I could have some dry clothes and we could talk about this someplace other than the bathroom?"

"Dry clothes? I haven't got—sure. Stay right here and I'll bring you something to put on."

Fred walked out of the bathroom with me.

"I'm locking the door so you can't escape until I get back," I called to Rick.

"Like I'm going anywhere soaking wet!"

Fred studied the ancient knob. "There's no lock on this door."

"I know. And I don't have any dry clothes for Rick. How long do you think it'll take him to figure all that out?"

We headed downstairs. "Long enough for a fresh batch of cookies, at least," he said.

"Speaking of locks, how did you get in here?"

"Through the front door."

"That door does have a lock, a strong deadbolt, and I locked it when I came in."

"I know."

"You heard me scream?"

"Yes."

Super hearing as well as x-ray vision.

I checked the front door as we went past and found it unlocked. Apparently he wasn't able to walk through walls. "Easier to unlock them than relock them?" I asked as I flipped the lock mechanism.

"Takes more time, and I was worried you were in danger since I heard you scream."

"Good call."

We went to the kitchen where Henry was still snoozing happily.

I took out some frozen cookie dough and a pan. "Apparently during the term of his demise, Rick's been spying on me," I said, tilting my head in Henry's direction. "He gave Henry catnip."

Fred sat down at the table. "Remember that night Marissa and her boys were here and I thought I saw one of them outside looking in the window?"

I shuddered. "Yes, I remember. Oh! You think it was Rick?"

He nodded.

I moved the roast to one side of the oven and slid the cookies in beside it then sat down on a chair next to Fred. "That's disgusting, but it explains some things. I've had this creepy feeling whenever I've been with Trent that Rick was watching us. Like one night we were on the porch, and I heard an animal hissing in the bushes. I thought I was just being paranoid, but I'll bet that was him, spying on me!" I slammed my fist onto the solid wood of the table. "I'm going to kill him. Everybody already thinks he's dead so I should be able to get away with it."

Fred shook his head. "You probably shouldn't do that. The police have doubts about his being in that explosion. They can't be far behind me. They'll find that bank account, discover that he took out money after he was supposed to be dead, and track him to that condo before long."

"That sucks."

"I know."

I had just taken the cookies out of the oven when we heard Rick pounding on the bathroom door. The cookies were cool enough to transfer from the pan to a rack before he figured out the door wasn't locked and came downstairs wearing his wet clothes and a frown.

"Very funny." He plopped down into a chair at the table.

"About as funny as you spying on me." I eyed the marble rolling pin sitting on the counter. If I were to whack Rick upside the head, I was pretty sure Fred wouldn't tell.

"I was looking out for my interests," Rick protested. "You've been hanging around with that cop like you were a single woman!"

"I was until a few minutes ago!" I leaned forward, wishing my words were bullets.

"No, you weren't! I didn't sign the divorce papers, and I wasn't dead!" He leaned toward me, looking smug.

Fred pushed us both back. "Entertaining as it is to listen to you two argue, I'd really like to ask you some questions, Rick, beginning with, who tried to kill you?"

Rick ran a hand through his damp hair and blew out a long breath. "I don't know. It could be one of several people."

"No surprise there." I rose and transferred the still-warm cookies to a plate. I thought about dividing them on two plates, one for Fred and one for me, but my mother's manners kicked in, and I set the single plate in the middle of the table. Of course Rick took one. With any sort of luck, it would be the cookie that contained the one chocolate chip that had been infused with a deadly poison before leaving the factory. But if I'd had that sort of luck, he'd have stayed dead in the first place.

"Are you making a roast?" Rick asked. "Something sure does smell good. I haven't had a decent meal since I've been on the run."

"Pizza Hut still delivers."

Fred cleared his throat. "I understand a lot of people probably wanted you dead, but do you have reason to suspect anyone in particular? Have there been threats?"

Rick took a bite of cookie. "Sure. I get those a lot. It goes with the business."

"Who threatened you recently?"

"Julia's husband, of course."

"Of course," I said. "It goes with the business."

"He's a jerk. Abuser. Used to beat the crap out of her. Hey, a woman doesn't cheat on her husband if she's got a good relationship at home."

I lifted an eyebrow but decided I'd just file and save that comment for the next time he accused me of cheating on him with Trent.

"That's why Julia came to me with the information about the highway extension. She wanted to divorce Akin, but when she talked to a lawyer, he told her she wouldn't get anything. Akin made her sign a pre-nup, and he was really careful to keep his money hidden. Seems his first wife got a big settlement and he was determined that wasn't going to happen again. So Julia and I had a business deal that she'd give me the information, and I'd split the profits with her."

I arched an eyebrow. "A business deal?"

He shrugged. "We got involved personally too. It just happened."

"Who else?" Fred asked, interrupting the discussion of Rick's love life.

"Bryan Kollar."

"Because you wouldn't sell him back his parents' property?"

"Yeah. He said I'd be sorry if I didn't sell it back to him. Said his parents wanted it because it's been in the family for generations, but I'm no fool. He must have found out about the..." He stopped in midsentence and looked at each of us in turn.

"The shopping center," I finished for him. "Old news. Go on."

"Albert Mayfield."

"Who's that?"

"Oh, we were involved in a project that didn't work out, and he got all upset about it."

"Let me guess. He threatened you when he lost a lot of money but somehow you made a profit."

"I'm good at what I do. Not everybody is. If they don't know what they're doing, they should stay out of the game."

"Who else?"

"Franklin Murdock."

"Wife or business deal?"

Rick shrugged. "Both."

"What about your mother? She ever threaten you?"

"Marissa?" He gave a short, cynical laugh. More of a snort, actually. "On a regular basis."

"How about more recently when you wouldn't let her in on your shopping center deal?"

"Oh, that. Sure, she carried on and made all kinds of threats. But she would never try to kill me.

140

Would she?" The last bite of cookie seemed to stick in his throat. "Can I have a glass of water?"

"Get it yourself. I'm sure you know where I keep the glasses if you know where I keep the catnip."

He glanced at Henry. "I had to do something! That cat acted like he was going to tear me apart."

"He would have if you hadn't drugged him. You just need to be sure you aren't still here when those drugs wear off."

"About that. I need to stay here until they catch my killer."

"You don't have a killer because you're not dead, and you're not staying here."

"I don't have a killer *yet*, but I will if you don't help me!"

"And why do you think I'd help you stay alive?"

"Because you're my—"

"Don't start with the *wife* crap again!" I shot up out of my chair and grabbed the rolling pin.

Fred stood and took it from me. "Don't do anything rash," he advised, guiding me back to my chair. "Rick, I think you can see that it would not be a good idea for you to stay here. What's wrong with the condo where you've been staying?"

"I think he's found me. I've seen somebody in a dark sedan sitting outside, and when I leave, he follows me."

I frowned. "I saw a dark sedan with its lights out going down my street a few nights ago."

"Oh, that was me," Rick admitted. "That's my temporary car, just a used one I paid cash for after mine got blown up."

A temporary car that he paid cash for?

141

I started to get up and grab the rolling pin again. Fred laid a hand on my arm and shook his head. Sometimes he can be really annoying.

"Hey," I said, "I got a great idea. Why don't you go back to your house? With all the people there, you'll be safe."

Rick flinched. "I can't believe you let those people in my house. They've probably destroyed it by now."

"Those people are your family. Your mother, your brothers, Grace, and your son."

Rick's eyes became narrow slits. "That rotten boy is not my son," he said through clenched teeth.

"As soon as we get the results of the DNA test back, we'll let you know."

Rick shook his head. "You don't have to do that. There's no way that kid is mine. For one thing, he doesn't look anything like me."

"He looks like his mother. That happens. You don't get to dictate which physical traits your children inherit."

Rick reached for another cookie and smiled. "Sometimes, you do. I had a vasectomy. I never told you because you wanted to have kids."

"A vasectomy? Why do I not believe that? You'd have been awfully young to have one of those before Rickie was born."

He shrugged. "I was seventeen, Mike was sixteen and Dan was fifteen."

"What?"

"Oh, that's right, you know them as Brad and Clint."

"I know who Mike and Dan are. But why would three teenage boys have vasectomies? What reputable doctor would do that?"

"A friend of Marissa's."

"Your mother..." I couldn't finish the sentence.

"After Dad left. She didn't want to take any chances, said we were enough to take care of. She didn't want any grandkids. We were all pretty wild."

"Where's your father now?"

"I don't know."

"Liar."

He glared at me.

A knock sounded on the front door.

Rick shot to his feet, perspiration breaking out on his forehead. Or maybe it was still his hair dripping. "He's here!"

"Who?" Fred asked.

"I don't know! Whoever it is that's trying to kill me!"

"I think it's probably Trent," I said, rising.

Rick grabbed my arm. "Don't let him in!"

I shook him off. "I invited him here. I didn't invite you. Why don't you just go out the back door and head over to your condo?"

"No," Fred said. "Rick, you need to talk to Trent. If you want the authorities to catch the man or woman who's threatening your life, you need to work with them."

"No way! I don't want anything to do with the cops, especially not my wife's lover."

"I told you not to start that *wife* crap again!" I kicked his shin.

"Ouch!"

"You have a choice, Rick," Fred said. "You can leave by the back door, get in your car, drive away and hope for the best, or you can talk to Trent and ask the police for their help."

I went toward the living room, hoping Rick would be gone when I returned with Trent.

When I opened the front door I found Trent standing on the porch, smiling, happy, anticipating a night of fun and frivolity.

"Rick's alive."

He stopped smiling. "That explains why we haven't been able to find his DNA in the remains from the explosion."

Two men who supposedly cared about me, and both of them babbled about DNA instead of the impact of this tragedy on my life. "Thanks for the sympathy." I turned away and headed back to the kitchen.

Henry still slept peacefully in the corner, a cat smile on his lips as catnip dreams played through his head. Other than that, the room was empty.

Rick, Fred and all the cookies were gone.

Chapter Seventeen

I let out a deep sigh and flopped into a chair, relieved Rick was gone but distressed I couldn't produce him for Trent. "He was here, I swear he was. Rick and Fred were sitting at this table eating my cookies when you knocked on the door."

Trent walked over to stand behind me, his strong fingers kneading my shoulder muscles. "Relax. Tell me what happened."

I considered my options. Burst into tears or make more cookies. I still had plenty of dough. But for the moment I decided to sit there and let Trent massage my knotted shoulders while I told him about Rick's near-death experience.

When I got to the part about Rick tossing his wallet out after the car exploded, Trent's fingers clenched. "That's the piece of evidence we withheld, the piece of evidence that anonymous caller gave us the other night when I had to leave you to meet with a man who never showed up."

My own fingers clenched, imagining them wrapped around Rick's throat. "That worthless creep. It was him. Rick was your anonymous caller who jacked you around all night. He just wanted to keep you and me apart."

Trent sat down in the chair next to me and took my hands in his. He looked every inch a cop now. "We need to find Rick. We've got to bring him in and question him. He has information that could help us find this killer."

I shook my head. "There are a lot of people who threatened him, but he doesn't know which one tried to kill him."

"We need to get all that information from him, and…" He cleared his throat and shifted in his chair then looked me squarely in the eye. "Now that we know Rick wasn't in the explosion, we have to consider him a suspect."

It took a moment for the full import of Trent's words to sink in. "You think Rick might have killed that woman?"

"At this point, I have no opinion one way or the other. But it happened at his house to his car and he somehow miraculously escaped while a woman died. That makes him an automatic suspect."

"Rick's good at that. Escaping while everybody around him goes up in flames, I mean."

"You said Fred was with Rick when you left them to answer the door."

"Yes. Sitting where you're sitting, eating cookies from that plate." That reminded me of my dinner plans. "Do you want some roast?"

Trent blinked a couple of times at the abrupt change of subject. "What?"

"I made a roast. It should be done. And I can make another pan of cookies in ten minutes. I have plenty of dough. We might as well eat. Rick's gone back into hiding. You're not going to find him tonight."

Trent released my hands and sat back in his chair. The expression on his face told me we weren't going to have an intimate dinner and a cozy evening together. He pulled out that ubiquitous pen and small notebook. "Do you have Fred's phone number?"

"Of course I do." I did not like the direction this conversation had taken.

Trent's jaw clenched. In a few minutes he'd be at the teeth-grinding stage. Well, I was already there. It was only fair that he share my frustration. "Would you please give me Fred's phone number?"

"No."

"No?"

"No. If Fred wanted you to have his phone number, he'd have given it to you."

Trent frowned. "Lindsay, this is official police business. I need to call Fred and see if he knows where Rick went."

I folded my arms obdurately. "Get a warrant if you want me to give you Fred's phone number."

Trent's frown deteriorated into a scowl, and his lips got tight. "I can call someone at the station and have them get that number for me in five minutes."

"Go for it." I stood, turned my back on him, took out my cookie sheet and cookie dough and began preparing to bake again.

"Lindsay, don't you want us to find Rick before the killer does?"

I considered that question while I slid the cookies into the oven and took out the roast. "I wouldn't mind going back to being a widow."

Nevertheless I picked up my cell phone and sat down at the table. I didn't want the Karma cops coming after me. I punched Fred's speed dial number.

"Do you know where Rick is?" I asked as soon as he answered.

"Yes, he's in the car in front of me."

I looked at Trent and nodded. He picked up the pen and poised it over the paper.

"Where are you?"

"In the vehicle behind Rick. I checked his car for bombs, and now I'm following him to his condo where I'll check for possible assailants then show him how to check his car each morning. If he'd had that knowledge last week, Julia might still be alive."

"That's nice of you, especially considering you don't like Rick, but Trent's here, and he wants to talk to him."

"I'll ask Rick to call Trent as soon as we arrive at the condo."

I moved the phone away from my mouth and spoke to Trent. "Fred will have Rick call you when they get to the condo."

Trent shook his head. "Not good enough. Where is the condo?"

"Fred, do you have the address for the condo?"

"Of course," Fred replied, "but I'm not going to share it with Trent at this time."

"Oh."

"Rick and I have reached an agreement. We'll keep him safe, help the police find the killer, and he'll sign the divorce papers as soon as the murderer is in jail."

I smiled. That explained why Fred was helping Rick. He was doing it for me. Fred was my friend. "Thank you! I appreciate that. I'll tell Trent."

I disconnected the call and passed along Fred's information to Trent. Not to my surprise, he wasn't happy.

The timer on my oven dinged. I took the cookies out and turned to Trent. "I have prepared a delicious meal. Why don't we just sit down and eat and have a nice evening together?"

Trent clenched his teeth again. I should talk to his dentist about giving me a cut of the man's dental bills. After all, a lot of it was my doing. "Lindsay, you have given me important information concerning an ongoing murder investigation. I can't just ignore that. I have to call it in."

I spread my hands in a gesture of resignation. "Okay. Call it in. Then we'll eat." I went to the cabinet and took down two plates.

Trent went to the other room and called somebody. I wasn't really trying to eavesdrop, but I wasn't trying not to, either, especially when I heard him ask the person on the other end to find a phone number for Fred Sommers.

He came back and sat down at the table. "This looks good." He didn't sound sincere.

"I tasted it. Everything is good."

He ate a few bites before he finally laid down his fork. "Why can't the department find Fred's phone number?"

I paused with a bite of roast halfway to my mouth. "I'm going to take a wild guess on that one. Because he doesn't want you to have it."

"Nobody can hide their phone number from the police."

I shrugged, ate the bite of roast and put a big dollop of sour cream on my pieces of onion and potatoes. "Whatever you say."

Trent resumed eating, but he didn't resume smiling or looking happy.

Rick had effectively ruined another evening for Trent and me. Taking into consideration that he likely made the anonymous call that got Trent out of the house the night before, I wondered if that had been the purpose of Rick's recent visit, to see that Trent and I didn't spend the night together. Was he really worried about an unknown mystery man stalking him or was he just determined to spoil my fun?

❧

Trent left early that evening, of course. We parted on good terms, but not nearly as good as they would have been had Rick not interfered in our evening.

Henry was awake by then and followed us outside. As Trent drove down the street, I waved then went to Fred's house, passing Henry where he lay in the grass. I stopped and looked down at him.

"You've got a problem," I told him. "Are you aware that, while you were lying in the kitchen zonked out on catnip, Rick was upstairs hiding in my shower?"

He looked chagrined...or hung over. I wasn't sure which.

I went on to Fred's house. He opened the door before I had a chance to knock or ring the bell.

"I've been expecting you," he said.

150

I walked inside. "Why can't the cops find your phone number?"

"They don't need it."

Made sense to me.

I went over to his sofa and sat down. He had been expecting me. A glass of white wine waited on the coffee table.

"I figured you'd need something to help you relax after Rick's stunt." He sat in the recliner and lifted his half-empty glass.

I sipped the wine. I'd have liked to chug it and ask for more, but it was too good. I sipped and enjoyed. "Do you think Rick really believes somebody's out to get him?"

"I actually think he does, though I found no evidence to support that belief. Once someone has tried to kill you, I suppose it's normal to be concerned they'll try again."

I swirled my wine, admiring the refraction of the light in the cut crystal. "And the list of possible suspects is long."

"We'll start on that list tomorrow."

I looked up. "We will?"

"If you want him to sign those papers, we will."

I nodded. "May I have more wine?"

"Certainly." He took both our glasses to the kitchen and refilled them then returned. "Tomorrow we'll talk to Akin's detective."

"What shall I wear?"

Fred considered that for a moment. "Something that makes you look vulnerable. Don't wear any makeup. Do you have a dress?"

"I have an old denim shirtwaist I haven't worn in a few years. It's faded, and the sleeves are a little frayed."

"That'll work. Do you have a wig?"

"No."

"I'll bring you one. Would you rather be blond or brunette?"

This could be interesting. Maybe not as entertaining as pretending to be a stripper, but interesting.

Chapter Eighteen

I have no idea how Fred convinced Ross Hamilton, Akin's private investigator, to talk to us, especially on a Sunday afternoon. I can only speculate that Fred had something on the man or he used Vulcan mind control. I didn't ask. I donned my faded denim dress, pulled my hair back and waited for Fred to bring a wig. It was long, blond and straight. I put it on and decided immediately I never wanted to be a blonde. With my already pale skin, I looked like a ghost who's spent at least a hundred years in a dungeon far away from the sun.

Hamilton's office was located in North Kansas City on the back side of a strip mall which had a chiropractor, a dentist and a title company on the front side. The sign on the door of the small office simply read *Hamilton & Associates.* Everything about the place was low-key and discreet, the sort of PI somebody with a high profile would feel comfortable hiring.

A man of medium height and weight with medium brown hair opened the door to Fred's knock and extended a hand. "Mr. Sommers? I'm Ross Hamilton." He had the kind of face that could disappear in a crowd. Low-keyed and discreet. In the jeans and knit shirt he wore that day, he looked like the guy next door. In a blue uniform, he'd probably look like a delivery guy. In work clothes, he could pass for the cable man or phone repair guy.

Fred shook his hand then turned to me. "This is my assistant, Diana Lindsay."

Hamilton studied me a moment before offering to shake my hand. "Have we met before?"

"I don't think so." Suddenly I understood the wig. Hamilton had been following Rick who'd been stalking me. Add to that my recent television appearance, and it was likely Hamilton had seen me. I moved past him, ducking my head and letting the blond hair fall over my face.

He invited us to sit in his low-key, discreet beige client chairs and offered us coffee. Fred refused because he's so persnickety about his coffee, and I refused because I don't like coffee. He didn't offer a Coke. We Coke drinkers are often discriminated against.

Hamilton took a seat behind his wooden desk. The surface was uncluttered except for a phone and his cup of coffee. He took a sip of the coffee then sat back and folded his arms. "So Rick Kramer's alive, and you're representing him?"

"That's correct."

"Do you have some identification?"

Fred took out his wallet and withdrew his driver's license, a business card and a card showing he was a member of the Missouri State Bar. I almost choked when I saw that last. Impersonating an insurance adjuster or an agent looking for strippers is one thing, but my dad's a lawyer, and I know that they get more than a little irate when somebody goes around impersonating an attorney.

Hamilton kept the business card and handed the others back to Fred. "I'm not legally bound to tell you anything about my investigation."

"If you don't want to answer my questions, I understand. Anything you do tell me will be kept completely confidential. My client is in fear for his life. Whatever information you can provide about what you might have seen while you had him under surveillance would be greatly appreciated."

Hamilton studied us quietly for several moments. Fred studied him back. I fidgeted.

"I wasn't there the morning of the explosion," Hamilton said. "I'd already concluded my investigation and turned everything over to Akin."

"Are you aware that Julia Akin called the police on four occasions to report physical abuse by her husband?"

"I was not aware of that. Mr. Akin hired me to find out if his wife was cheating on him. That's all I was concerned with."

Fred nodded slowly. "I understand. And you turned your report over to Mr. Akin before the murder took place?"

"Yes, I did. Almost a week before."

"I see. Does it bother you that you may have provided information that got Mrs. Akin killed?"

"I did the job I was hired to do." Hamilton's voice was calm and even, as though he were discussing the weather, but his jaw tightened and his lips firmed. I did not think he was as unaffected as he wanted us to believe.

Fred sat silently. Hamilton took another sip of coffee. A sheen of sweat broke out on his forehead.

"It doesn't look good for Akin," Fred said. "His first wife charged him with abuse, but she dropped the charges after she got a hefty settlement."

That sheen of sweat spread to Hamilton's upper lip. He cleared his throat. "I wasn't involved in that case."

"I understand. Not part of your job. And the abuse was never proven."

We all sat in silence for a moment while Hamilton's sweat factor ramped up.

"When Mr. Akin hired you to follow his wife, did he tell you what he planned to do with the information if you found that she was having an affair?"

Hamilton wrapped his fingers tightly around his coffee cup. "He discovered she was talking to a lawyer about a divorce. He said his first wife took him for everything, and he didn't intend for that to happen again. If he could get proof of infidelity, he'd have a bargaining chip."

"So he was okay with the divorce, just concerned about the financial aspect of it?"

Hamilton nodded, sitting straighter in his chair. "I get a lot of cases like that. If one spouse can prove the other one's cheating, it gives them better leverage in the divorce. Akin wanted to be prepared so as soon as she filed, he could file a countersuit and charge her with adultery."

"Divorce. Legal action." Fred nodded slowly. "Mr. Akin had a pre-nup with his wife. Why did he need further leverage?"

Hamilton's fingers twitched slightly as he picked up his coffee cup and lifted it to his lips, taking a sip then setting it back on the desk. If it had been full, he'd have sloshed coffee onto that desk. "I was hired to do a job. The client's motives are none of my business."

"Of course. Did he threaten his wife? Show any signs of violence when he talked about her?"

Hamilton licked his lips and shook his head. "No. He was always calm and controlled, not a man you'd associate with abuse."

"Abusers often show a different side to everybody except their victims. My assistant was married to an abusive man. She's one of the lucky ones. She escaped with her life."

I tried to look vulnerable.

"I'm sorry," Hamilton said. "Good thing you got away from him. Not all women do."

He swallowed, his Adam's apple bobbing as he apparently realized what he'd said. He took another sip of coffee. His hand shook.

"I shot him," I said, wanting to contribute something to the conversation.

Hamilton's eyes widened and Fred choked, turning the sound into a cough.

Well, he should have given me a script.

"While you had Mrs. Akin and Mr. Kramer under surveillance, did you observe anything suspicious, anyone else who might be watching either him or her?" Fred asked, changing the subject. Guess he didn't like my ad-lib.

Hamilton sat silently for a long moment before he finally spoke. "One night I observed Mr. Kramer fighting with another woman on his front porch while Mrs. Akin was inside his house."

I leaned forward, waiting to hear the rest of the story. It did not surprise me that Rick would cheat on Julia. Duh.

"Can you describe the incident in more detail?"

Hamilton tented his fingers and seemed relieved to be discussing something other than his guilt in Julia Akin's murder. After practically being accused of being an accomplice to murder, he was probably willing to spill his guts about anything that would make him seem less guilty.

"Mr. Akin was out of town and I followed Mrs. Akin to Mr. Kramer's house. She'd been inside for about an hour when another car pulled into the driveway and a woman got out."

"Can you describe the woman?"

"Blond hair, medium height, very...umm...pretty."

From the way he spread his hands in the vicinity of his chest, I figured *pretty* meant *triple D*.

"She rang the doorbell. Mr. Kramer answered and tried to close the door in her face, but she stuck her purse in the opening and yelled at him."

"Could you hear what she yelled at him?"

"No. I was too far away, and I didn't have any sound equipment set up. Mr. Akin just asked for pictures."

Fred nodded. "Go on."

"Mr. Kramer came out on the porch, and the two of them got into it. At first she was smiling and trying to talk to him, but he just kept shaking his head, and that seemed to make her mad. Soon she started hitting him. Punched him in the stomach a couple of times then whacked him in the face with that purse. I figured he'd smack her, but he didn't. Just put up his hands to protect himself, then ran back in the house. She rang the doorbell and knocked for a long time, but he never came back to the door. I figured it was a former girlfriend though she looked a little older than him, one of those women who work at not looking their age. She was wearing a lot of makeup, and she had long red fingernails."

Marissa was a little older, wore too much makeup, had long red fingernails and she'd certainly smacked Clint and Brad. If it had been a former girlfriend, Rick would have at least grabbed her arms to stop her hitting him. I was glad to know he showed a little respect for his mother, whether or not she deserved it.

"Do you remember what kind of car she was driving?"

"It was an old Honda Civic."

Marissa was now driving a Cadillac, but it was rented.

"Did you get the license plate off that Civic?"

"Yes."

The man was putty in Fred's hands. He might not want to tell him everything, but he would, if pressed.

"Did you run the plates?"

"They came back to some woman who lives in Crappie Creek. I don't remember the name off the top of my head. Melissa, something like that. I turned in my report shortly after that, and my client wasn't interested in her identity."

Melissa, Marissa, Mary. Had to be Mama.

"Do you know who Bryan Kollar is?" Fred asked.

Hamilton appeared puzzled at the question. "Of course. Everybody around here knows who Bryan Kollar is."

"Did you see him with Mr. Kramer at any time?"

"No. Were the two of them buddies?"

"They were involved in a business deal. Did you ever, during the time you had Mrs. Akin or Mr. Kramer under surveillance, notice a dark blue Jaguar parked in the area or driving by?"

He shook his head. "No. I'd have noticed a car like that. In my job, I have to notice everything."

Fred nodded and stood. Hamilton and I stood too. Hamilton looked relieved that the interview was at an end.

"I very much appreciate your sharing your information with us." Fred stepped forward and extended a hand across Hamilton's desk.

They shook, then I took Hamilton's hand. It was damp. Yeah, the man would be glad to see us leave.

"Did he die?" Hamilton asked.

"Rick?" Fred looked surprised at the question. "No, he's still alive. He's my client."

"I know that. I meant her husband." He tilted his head toward me. "The one she shot."

"No," Fred said firmly. "She's a lousy shot."

I smiled vulnerably.

Actually, I smiled through clenched teeth. Fred would pay for that remark.

Chapter Nineteen

My first question as we were slowly wending our way down Interstate 29 in Fred's car was, "Can I take off this wig?"

"By all means. Don't ever go blond. You're too pale."

"Thank you for that bit of advice." I pulled off the wig and tossed it into the back seat then glared at him. He didn't notice. "Who drives a blue Jaguar? Bryan Kollar?"

"Yes. I was hoping we'd get a hit on him, but that's a pretty hard car to miss."

"Maybe he has a secret car, something not quite so flashy for when he's stalking people he plans to kill."

"Maybe."

We rode in silence for a couple of minutes. It's difficult for me to go long without saying something. "I've got some advice for you. You shouldn't have let Hamilton keep that business card saying you're a lawyer. I'm pretty sure impersonating a lawyer is a crime."

Fred continued to stare out the windshield, showing no signs of fear at my dire warning. "If you represent yourself as a lawyer and dispense legal advice, you can be charged with a crime. I dispensed no legal advice and I did actually pass the Missouri, Kansas and Oklahoma bar exams."

"Oh." It was the only thing I could think of to say. Time for a change of subject. "So where are we headed now? To confront Akin? Do you think he did it?"

"I think it's very possible. I'd like to find out if he knew that Julia told Rick about the highway deal. Eventually we'll talk to him, but right now I thought we might spend Sunday afternoon with the family."

I turned to look at him in shock and horror. "You want to go to my parents' house? Are you sure?"

"Wrong family. I'm talking about Rick's family."

I sat back. "Okay, I guess I'm up for that. Are you going to tell them Rick's alive?"

"No."

"You told Hamilton."

"We don't have to worry about Hamilton telling anybody. Right now he's so guilt-ridden about his possible involvement in a death that he's going to have bad dreams for a month. He's really too sensitive for that job."

"If Marissa's the one who tried to kill Rick and we tell her that he's still alive, she might try again."

"Pull in your fangs and stop smiling at that idea."

I sighed and watched the scenery roll slowly by for a few minutes. "Can we stop by my house and get my camera first so I can take pictures of the devastation at Rick's house?"

"Use your phone."

"My camera has higher resolution. It'll provide Rick with a better image of all the gruesome details."

"Our goal is not to get pictures of all the gruesome details. Our goal is to figure out who tried to kill Rick so he'll sign your divorce papers."

"You're right. For a moment I lost sight of that goal in the anticipation of seeing Rick's house wrecked."

"There's no reason you shouldn't enjoy the journey to your goal."

"So we can go by for the camera?"

"No. We don't want to arrive too late."

"Then drive faster."

He didn't.

෨෴෧

Rick's yard was decorated with bright orange, gold and red plastic toys. I was sure the neighbors Rick was always trying to impress would be duly impressed with that.

Marissa answered the door. She looked less than perfect, a little frazzled, but she managed a big phony smile. "Lindsay, how nice to see you again. And Mr. Sommers. I wasn't expecting you."

"Sorry we didn't call first." Fred gave her an equally phony smile. "Lindsay just wanted to see if you were settling in okay, finding everything."

A crash sounded from somewhere behind Marissa. She whirled around and headed back inside. "What has that damn kid broken now?"

Fred indicated the open door. "After you."

I crossed the foyer into the living room.

Rickie stood in the middle of the living room looking down at Rick's marble chess pieces and the remnants of what used to be a very ugly but very expensive vase. The champagne beige carpet was

163

now more mud and other unknown substances than champagne. One drape sagged from a bent rod, and the other had been ripped halfway across. The fireplace tongs lay in two pieces on the hearth, and the corner of one of the stones on that hearth had been broken off. The Pueblo Suede paint on the walls had proven to be a suitable background for several crayon scrawls. I took out my cell phone and snapped a couple of pictures to share with Rick.

"It wasn't my fault!" Rickie whined. "It was an accident!"

"You little monster!" Marissa shrieked, seizing the child by one arm.

"Leave him alone!" Grace charged up and grabbed Marissa's arm.

Marissa turned her attention to her attacker. "That brat has wrecked this place! Don't you have any control over him?"

"You mean the kind of control you have over your sons? You want me to slap him around like you do Mike and Dan? You think that's the right way to raise a child? You think it's right to send them upstairs to their rooms at their age?"

"After what they did yesterday, I believe the punishment was justified. You notice they did what I told them to do. My sons are a lot better behaved than yours!" Marissa leaned forward, getting in Grace's face. "But what chance did that demon child have anyway with Kenneth Reardon for a father?"

Grace slapped Marissa.

Marissa grabbed a handful of Grace's hair and yanked.

Rickie moved to one side of the room and picked up Rick's crystal wine decanter. Apparently fascinated with the rainbow refractions, he moved it around in the late afternoon sunlight streaming through the window past the torn drapes.

Grace and Marissa scratched, punched, pulled and cursed.

I took pictures.

"I guess we'd better stop them." Fred took a step in the direction of the fight.

I put out an arm to halt him. "Do we have to?"

"If we want to talk to them."

"Fine, go ahead. But I was really hoping to see a little blood."

"Ladies…" Fred pushed the women apart and held them firmly. "I feel certain we can resolve this without resorting to physical violence."

"How dare you say that about Kenneth being Rickie's daddy right in front of him?" Grace demanded, struggling to free herself from Fred's grip. "How can you hurt your own grandson like that, you bitch?"

"Because that little demon is *not* my grandson! Kenneth may not be his father. I have no idea how many other men you slept with, and you probably don't either! But I know one thing for certain, my son did not father that brat!"

The sound of breaking glass interrupted the insult fest. Rickie stood beside the fireplace looking down at the shattered decanter on the stone hearth. "I didn't mean to do it," he whined.

Grace raced over to him. "Be careful you don't cut yourself."

165

"He's going to destroy everything in this house!" Marissa shouted.

Grace wrapped an arm around Rickie's thin shoulders and glared at Marissa. "So what if he does? It's his house!"

At that moment I would have liked to tell them Rick was still alive and neither one of them was getting a penny, but I held my tongue and kept taking pictures. I could do some sort of a collage for Rick. He'd so enjoy it. Okay, maybe he wouldn't enjoy it, but I'd enjoy watching him not enjoy it.

"Ladies, can we sit down and talk for a few minutes?" Fred actually appeared a little frazzled. "There are some things about Rick's estate that we need to discuss."

Marissa jabbed a hand through the air toward Grace. "Talk to her while she cleans up the messes her brat made. I've got to get dressed. Bryan's coming to take me to dinner."

"That's disgusting!" Grace said. "He's young enough to be your son."

Marissa smiled and arched a perfect eyebrow. "But he's not my son. Jealous because you can't even find an old man who wants you?"

Grace stooped and began picking up the larger pieces of broken crystal. Rickie turned on the big screen television. "Bryan doesn't want you," Grace snapped. "He just wants the property he thinks you're going to own."

"And he's willing to pay me a lot of money for the property I'm going to own as soon as my son's estate is settled. Will you turn that television down? Are you deaf?"

166

Rickie changed the channel but made no move to turn down the volume.

"How much money is he going to pay you?" Fred asked, flinching from the loud commercial.

Marissa's smile widened as she quoted the figure. "We've already signed an Intent to Sell, so he has no reason to take me to dinner except that he likes my company."

"What about the shopping center?" I asked. "Wouldn't you make more money on that if you kept the property?"

She gave an indolent shrug. "Why be greedy? Besides, I don't know the first thing about putting together a shopping center. I plan to sell all those properties."

"What happens to those properties will be up to Rick's son! I'll bet Bryan wouldn't be hanging around you so much if he knew that!" Grace charged over to where Fred and Marissa stood.

"Have you forgotten you tried to tell him that, and he didn't believe you? When that DNA test comes back, you're going to look pretty stupid."

Grace tossed the crystal remnants at Marissa. One barely missed Fred's cheek as he ducked. "You can take your DNA test and stick it! I'm not putting my son through something like that!" She grabbed Rickie's arm and stomped out of the room.

Marissa glared at their departing backs. "I'll be so glad when this is all over and that little bitch goes back to Crappie Creek where she belongs." She looked over at me. "When is that DNA test going to be finished?"

167

I looked at Fred, and she caught the direction of my gaze. She smiled up at Fred. "Any idea when this is going to be settled? When will we hear about the results of the DNA test?"

"Another day or two."

Marissa nodded. Now that I knew about the vasectomies, I realized why she was so confident Rickie was not Rick's son. "Have they caught my son's killer?" She batted her eyelashes at Fred.

"Not yet, but soon. They've got some strong leads."

"Good. Can you show yourselves out? I need to change." She started from the room.

"They know about the fight you and Rick had on his front porch," I said.

She stopped and turned back to look at me, her eyes narrowed. "How would anybody know about private discussions my son and I had?"

"Not so private when you're outside shouting. People saw, people heard, people told me."

"And I suppose you told that cop you're dating."

I shrugged. Obviously I was no longer her darling Lindsay. "You can suppose anything you want. Just be prepared when they come to question you."

She shot me a final glare and disappeared up the stairs.

Fred and I went out the door.

A dark blue Jaguar pulled into the driveway as we crossed the porch. Oh, yay. We were going to get to talk to Bryan again. Be still, my heart.

He got out of the car...smiling, of course. "Lindsay and Fred. Nice to see you again. Have you been visiting with Marissa?"

"Marissa and Grace and, of course, Rick's son," I said. "I understand you have an agreement with Marissa, but have you talked to Rickie about getting your parents' property back? Intestate dead person, half to the spouse and half to the lineal descendants, per stirpes. That means his only lineal descendant, Rickie."

He was so hot to get that property back, willing to pay an outrageous price for it, I just thought I'd rattle his chain, see what he'd do if he wasn't so sure the property was going to belong to Marissa. Okay, I was trying to stir up trouble. That smarmy man and those two women inside deserved some trouble.

Bryan's smile didn't falter as he climbed the steps to the porch. "Marissa assures me that boy is not Rick's son. The DNA test will prove it."

"Yes, the DNA will prove one way or the other if he's Rick's son." Fred and I started down the steps, then I stopped and looked back. "I was married to Rick. I know the truth about that boy's parentage."

Bryan's smile was still locked in place, but it looked pretty tight. Oh, yeah, there'd be trouble in Kansas City tonight.

Fred and I walked out to his car.

"That was clever," he said, pulling into the street. "It will be interesting to see what Bryan does if he's no longer so certain he's going to get that property. The more stressed he is the more likely he is to slip up, make a mistake."

169

I nodded and decided not to tell him I did it just for fun, to provoke another cat fight.

"Let's stop and pick up some burgers and onion rings on the way home," I said.

"We're not going home just yet. We have one more stop. I want to see what Bryan's parents think about this situation with their flour mill."

Chapter Twenty

We drove across town to a neighborhood of well-tended lawns with trees mature enough to suggest the houses had been there for twenty or thirty years. We parked down the street from a tidy gray home with tidy white trim and a tidy yard marred by "For Sale" and "Open House" signs linked together by a string of colorful flags.

"Is that where they live?" I asked.

"That is the residence of Walter and Alice Kollar, parents of Bryan Kollar."

"And we're going to go in there and tell those poor old people we're interested in buying their home, right?"

"I wouldn't refer to them as *poor old people*, but, yes, we're potential home buyers, Jim and Penny Richards."

"Where do you come up with these names? Did you write a special software program to create them?"

"Jim and Penny Richards are friends of mine, and they don't have a problem with my using their names."

"More friends? Are these real friends or just virtual people you've created on the computer?"

"Jim and Penny are real." I noticed he skirted around the possibility of some of his friends being virtual.

"Can I meet these people?"

"If we ever go to Las Vegas, yes, you can." He reached inside his pocket and withdrew a gold ring etched with strange characters. "Put this on."

I took the ring and looked at it curiously. "What does it say? What's that language?"

"It's the Black Speech of Mordor."

I almost dropped the ring. "This is the One Ring from Lord of the Rings?"

Fred sighed. "It's not the real thing. Put it on. You won't become invisible or be under its spell."

"I know that," I lied. "I'm just surprised you have something so fanciful, though you do bear some resemblance to a younger, better groomed Gandalf."

I slid the ring onto my finger then held my breath for a few seconds, waiting to see if I might disappear or develop an unnatural attachment to the ring. Considering who gave it to me, it actually could have been the real thing. With Fred, you just never know.

Nothing happened. I knew it wouldn't. Well, I was pretty sure it wouldn't.

A man and woman in shorts and tank tops jogged down the street and turned into the Open House. A strange way to preview houses. Perhaps an impulse look.

"What are we waiting for?" I asked, impatient to get on with things.

Fred checked his watch. "In a minute."

A woman wearing a dark suit and a badge that I felt sure identified her as a real estate agent emerged from the house followed by the joggers. They shook hands, and the agent took down the "Open House" sign along with the string of flags, got into the four door mid-sized car parked in the driveway and left. The joggers went back inside. Bryan's brother or sister?

"We're up." Fred opened his car door and got out.

"Who were those joggers? Are they caretakers for the Kollars?"

He was already out of the car and heading for my side to open the door. I got out and followed him.

The male jogger came to the door, still flushed from his run. Up close I could see that he had a few gray hairs, but he was in terrific shape...wiry and slim without an ounce of fat. "If you're here to see the house, our real estate agent just left."

"Darn," Fred said. *Darn?* Who knew that benign word was even in Fred's vocabulary? "We got stuck in traffic and just couldn't get here in time."

"And we were so anxious to see the place," I said, holding up my end of the story even though the last time I did, my contribution wasn't properly appreciated. "We just love this neighborhood."

The man smiled and stepped back, opening the door. "Come on in. You don't look like serial killers."

"Walter?" The female jogger came in from the kitchen holding two bottles of water. Up close she too had a few gray hairs in her pony tail, but I'd have killed to have a body with abs like hers.

"A couple of late arrivals to look at the house," the man said, turning to the woman.

173

"Jim and Penny Richards." Fred held out his hand.

The man took Fred's hand in a solid grip. "Walter and Alice Kollar."

What had Bryan said about his parents? *Elderly? Senile?*

Alice stepped forward, smiling. "Can I get you something to drink?"

"No, thanks," Fred said, declining for us both. Good grief. We'd only been married ten minutes and already he was speaking for me. I wouldn't have said no to a cold Coke. "We'd really appreciate a quick tour of the house, but we don't want to take up too much of your time."

"Don't be silly," Alice said, handing one of the bottles of water to her husband. "We just finished a five mile run, and we're in for the evening. You'll have to go through our real estate agent for any negotiations, but we'll be happy to show you our home. This, as you no doubt noticed, is the living room with wood-burning fireplace."

"We've burned a lot of wood in there," Walter said, glancing toward the stone structure. "I have the chimney cleaned every year. Never had a problem with it drawing properly, though I have to tell you, it doesn't do a thing to heat the place!" He chuckled at his own comment.

"But it looks nice," Alice said with a smile. "That's all modern fireplaces are supposed to do."

"It is beautiful," I agreed.

"Have you lived here long?" Fred asked as we strolled into the kitchen.

"Almost thirty years. We built the place," Walter said. "So we can assure you it's solid. Steel I-beams in the basement, no foundation problems."

"The cabinets are oak," Alice said, waving a hand about the spacious, airy kitchen. "All these appliances have been replaced at least once over the years, some a couple of times."

Fred opened cabinet doors and pretended to be interested. "This is a very nice home. Why are you selling?"

"We're retiring and plan to do a lot of traveling," Walter said.

"We love to run in marathons all over the country, so we thought we'd just get a small condominium close to our son and then we won't have to worry about the grass dying in the middle of August or what happens if our pipes freeze in Kansas City while we're running around Corpus Christi."

Elderly? Senile?

We toured the house and made the appropriate sounds of approval. It was a nice house, three bedroom, two bath, two car garage, finished basement with an extra half bath. Nothing fancy, but, as Walter said, *solid.* Well cared for. It was hard to imagine someone as flashy as Bryan Kollar growing up in that house.

Finally we returned to the living room and took seats on the comfortable sofa and matching loveseat facing the stone fireplace that looked pretty but didn't heat effectively.

"Where do you work?" Walter asked.

"I'm an actuary for Bremington Investments." Fred produced a card from his pocket and handed it to Walter.

Walter accepted the business card and looked at it. "You work right down the street. This would be a convenient location for you. Where do you live now?"

Fred gave a location across town. "Tired of all the driving."

Walter nodded. "I hear you. My sporting goods business is...was...located in the Bottoms. I had to fight all that downtown traffic for years."

"*Was?*"

Walter patted Alice's leg, and they both smiled. "Sold the business, selling the house, becoming mobile."

"Kollar," I said, rolling the name around on my tongue. "You had a sporting goods business? Are you related to Bryan Kollar?"

Alice smiled and nodded. "Our son. He's the reason we're able to do all this."

"He's very successful," I said. "That's great that he's willing to help his parents."

"Oh, no," Walter protested, "we'd never take money from Bryan. Alice just meant that he's the reason we opened the sporting goods store and started running. Changed our lives."

"It's hard to believe looking at him now," Alice said, "but Bryan was a sickly child. He's adopted, and we've often wondered about his birth mother, if she did something that got him off to a rough start in life. But practically overnight while he was in college, he got into vitamins and supplements and

176

working out, and then he opened his first gym." She smiled and lifted her hands. "And the rest is history."

Walter leaned back. "We were teachers and led a fairly sedentary lifestyle. But after we saw what happened with Bryan, we took up jogging, quit our jobs and opened the sporting goods store."

"That's amazing," I said. "He started his first gym right after he graduated?"

Alice shifted uncomfortably and looked at her husband. "Actually, he didn't graduate. He quit during his third year because he knew what he wanted to do and didn't see any reason to spend more time in school."

Fred gave a sad smile. "You're lucky. Our son's been in college for five years and still doesn't know what he wants to do." Married half an hour, and already we were parents of a grown son who showed signs of being a perennial student. "As far as I can tell, all he wants to do is call home for more money and go off to the next party."

Alice nodded, her expression sympathetic. "I know what you mean. Bryan went through that stage. His first couple of years in college, he got in with the wrong crowd, and we were pretty worried for a while. But then he got into weight lifting and all of a sudden he straightened up. He found his purpose in life. Your son will be fine. Look what a success Bryan made of himself."

"Did your son ever..." Fred's voice trailed off, and he dropped his gaze to the floor. I decided I'd better do the same thing since he was apparently about to confess something horrible our son had done. I felt guilty. Had we failed to give him enough

177

chocolate? "No, never mind," he said. "I'm sure Bryan Kollar would never have..." Fred swallowed then resumed speaking as if it was difficult to say the words. "Our son, we think he may be doing drugs."

I knew it! Chocolate deficit disorder!

Walter and Alice exchanged glances. "Don't worry," Walter reassured us. "It happens. It's a stage lots of kids go through."

"We're pretty sure Bryan was using...substances he shouldn't have been using," Alice said. "The crowd he got involved with...well, they weren't other college students. They were some pretty rough characters."

"How did you handle it?" I asked, trying to sound worried about my fictional son. I felt certain it was Fred's fault he'd gone astray. I had done my best to provide the boy with adequate chocolate.

"It was very scary," Alice said. "We just let him know we were there for him and we loved him no matter what but we didn't approve of his bad choices. It was a rough time. We got through it. You'll get through it."

"Thank you so much for sharing that with us," I said, feeling a little ashamed of myself for eliciting such personal information on a phony basis, but it was for a good reason. "It does help us to see how your story turned out. Your son's a success, and now you're going to retire thanks to selling the business your son inspired you to start."

"Well," Walter said, "that and the sale of an old flour mill that belonged to my great grandfather. Some real estate guy came along out of the blue and offered us more money for it than I'd ever have thought about. Gave us the extra boost we needed to retire."

Bryan's parents were not old or senile, and they didn't seem the least bit upset about selling the flour mill. Whatever reason Bryan had for wanting it back, it had nothing to do with his parents. Rick and his family weren't the only liars around.

The Kollars gave us their real estate agent's business card, and we promised to call her.

Okay, we lied, but Bryan started it.

శ్రా

"Our son?" I asked when we were back in the car and heading home. "You let them think I'm old enough to have a son who's been in college for five years?"

"You were precocious." He guided the car around a slow turn. "It worked. They admitted that their son had some problems, got in with the wrong crowd."

"Apparently he got away from that crowd. The man won't even eat sugar. I can't imagine him doing drugs."

"Body builders don't usually consider steroids in the same class as drugs."

I nodded. "It does sound like he bulked up pretty fast, and he is abnormally well developed. But what could that have to do with his obsession about that old flour mill or his possible involvement in Rick's murder?"

"I'm not sure. I'd like to find out more about the crowd he got involved with in college. I'd also like to find out where he got the money to open his first gym when he was still in school."

179

"Oh, good point. And what about his parents opening that sporting goods store? If they were both teachers and sending a son to college, it seems unlikely they'd have had the money to suddenly open a business. They said Bryan didn't help them, but maybe he loaned them some money and they paid him back and don't consider that *help*. Only place I can think of that a kid in college could get that kind of money would be selling drugs."

Fred grinned. "Very good. I was thinking the same thing. Maybe that ring has given you super powers after all."

I'd forgotten about The Ring. I looked down at my hand where it shone with a quiet glow. In the gathering dusk that came through the car windows, the characters almost seemed to move.

I touched it. The metal was warm.

Well, of course it was warm. It had been on my finger for an hour, and the temperature outside was in the eighties.

I yanked it off and handed it back to Fred. But I wouldn't feel comfortable until I got home and checked the mirror to be sure I still had all my hair and teeth.

Chapter Twenty-One

Monday arrived way too soon. I'd expected to be happily exhausted with a tired smile on my face after a wild weekend with Trent. Instead I'd had a wild weekend with Rick, his relatives and possibly his would-be murderers. Nevertheless, daybreak found me slinging Chocolate Chip Pancakes, and my No-Crust Chocolate Meringue Pie was a big hit at lunch.

It looked as if the day would pass as smoothly as my pie filling, but then the restaurant phone rang just as the lunch rush was ending. The noise burst into the room with a chilling intensity. Somehow I knew it wasn't the usual call about our hours or location.

The One Ring from Mordor. It had given me super powers after all. My hair had seemed unusually messy that morning.

Or it could be that I was expecting a disaster since we hadn't had one for more than twenty-four hours.

Paula was across the room serving pie to the last customers in the place, so I set my tray of dirty dishes on the counter and picked up the receiver. "Death by Chocolate. How can I help you?"

"Is Rickie there?"

I almost didn't recognize the subdued voice. "Grace?"

"Yes, it's me. Is Rickie with you?"

"Rickie? No, of course he's not here. Why on earth would you think he was here?"

"Has he been there today?"

"Not that I know of. Grace, have you mislaid your son?"

"Maybe."

I lifted a hand to my forehead. *Maybe?* "When did you see him last?"

"He wanted to stay up late last night because he was in the middle of some video game so I went to bed and let him play."

"*Last night?*" Paula and the couple with the pie all looked up when I practically shrieked the question. I turned my back to them and lowered my voice. "You haven't seen him since last night?"

"I wasn't worried at first. He wanders around by himself a lot. I figured it was a safe neighborhood." A defensive note crept into her usual nasal tone.

"Have you called the police?"

"No."

"Maybe you should do that," I said, trying to sound calm and not like I thought she was a total idiot. "He could be lost." *Or worse.* I thought of the time a year ago when Paula's psycho ex had kidnapped Zach. Paula had been hysterical. Grace was taking this pretty serenely.

"I don't want to call the police. I have some, uh, parking tickets."

"I don't care if there's a warrant out for your arrest for murder! Your son's missing. You need to call the cops."

Grace burst into sobs as if she suddenly comprehended the situation. "Can you please come over here?"

"You want me to come over there? Why me? Where are Marissa and her sons?"

"I don't know!" she wailed. "She told me Rickie probably ran away from home just to get away from me, and then they left! I'm all alone, and you're the closest thing to family I've got since you were married to my son's daddy."

More and more I was beginning to appreciate my own dysfunctional family even with all their dysfunctions.

"I can't leave here," I said. "I have a business to run."

I felt a hand on my shoulder and turned to see Paula standing behind me. "Go," she said quietly. "I can finish cleaning up. If her son's missing, she'll need somebody. I couldn't have made it without you and Fred when Zach disappeared."

I didn't think this was quite the same situation, but I didn't argue. "Grace, I'll be there as soon as I can, and you really need to call the police. Now!"

I hung up and explained the situation to Paula.

"She hasn't seen her son since last night?"

The people eating No-Crust Chocolate Meringue Pie looked up again at Paula's exclamation.

"No wonder he's such a brat," I said. "Who wouldn't be with a mother like Grace? I'll help clean and then I'll go over there."

"Go now. I can finish here, and I'll call Fred to see if he wants to meet you over there."

I hesitated.

"What if Henry was missing?" she said. "Wouldn't you want somebody to be there with you?"

I couldn't argue with that. I took my purse and left.

While I was stopped at a traffic light, I called Trent, got his voicemail and left a message.

Okay, it was a stop sign, but I have him on speed dial and I have a Bluetooth and he never answers anyway, so it wasn't really like I was talking on my phone while driving. And anyway, I wasn't speeding while I was doing it.

I arrived at Rick's house to find Grace pacing up and down on the sidewalk in front. She rushed up to me and grabbed my arms the minute I got out of my car. Grabby folk from Crappie Creek.

"Did you call the police?" I asked.

She nodded. "They're going to send somebody over."

"Good. In the meantime, let's go talk to the neighbors. Maybe somebody's seen him." I figured that would be a futile effort. Rick's neighbors...my former neighbors...made a concerted effort not to see anything. But it would give us something to do while waiting for the cops.

We'd been to three houses by the time the first officers arrived. Two people hadn't answered the door, and the other had given us a quick, cursory, "No," before closing the door in our faces.

Grace ran over to the officers as they got out of their car.

Fred pulled into the driveway, and I hurried to his car.

"Paula told you?" I asked.

He nodded, unfolded his lanky frame from the Mercedes and stepped out. "How's Grace taking it?"

"She's starting to freak out. I think it's finally hit her that something may have happened to the kid."

Fred turned to study Grace and the two officers as they led her down the sidewalk and into the house. "You know they always look at the parents first when a child disappears."

I nodded, recalling the way the cops had handled the situation when Zach was kidnapped.

Another cop car pulled up. The officers went inside the house then came back out almost immediately and went to the nearest neighbor's house. Those same people who hadn't answered my knock were suddenly home.

Fred opened a briefcase in the front seat of his car, took out what appeared to be a Bluetooth earpiece and stuck it in his ear. "Let's go for a walk," he said.

We strolled down the street, stopping to admire flowers along the way.

I knew what he was doing. Eavesdropping with the aid of a technical device. I wasn't certain if the technical device negated the stigma of bad manners, but I was certain I wanted one.

"What are they saying?" I demanded as the cops lingered at the door of the second house.

"Nothing yet."

I could tell by Fred's instantly alert expression when the cops hit pay dirt. I looked at the house and saw they were talking to a teenage boy who didn't look happy to be interacting with the police.

Fred took my arm and we strolled another few feet. "Tell me!" I ordered.

He leaned over to sniff the roses on a bush at the house next door to the one where the action was taking place, completely ignoring me.

Trent had a gun, Fred had all sorts of spy devices, and I had chocolate. Mine definitely tasted the best but gave me no advantage whatsoever with criminals.

"When this is over, I want my own earpiece," I said through gritted teeth. Should have kept The Ring. Maybe I could have used it to bargain with.

Fred smelled another rose.

The cops left that house, made a phone call, then backtracked and went to the house on the other side of Rick's.

Fred moved over to lean against a large oak tree. He wasn't smiling. I followed him. "That kid was talking on the phone to his girlfriend last night about 3:00 a.m. He was looking out his bedroom window while they talked, and he saw a van pull up in front of Rick's house. A tall man got out, went inside and came back almost immediately carrying a bundle over his shoulder."

I swallowed around the lump that suddenly came up in my throat. "A bundle of what?"

"It was dark, and he was paying more attention to his girlfriend than to the neighbors. But he said it was about four feet long and floppy, looked like something wrapped in a blanket. The kid said the man was carrying it over his shoulder like firemen carry people from a burning building in the movies. "

"Rickie didn't run away and he didn't wander off," I said quietly.

"No. Somebody took him, somebody who deliberately came after him. This was no random snatch. The man knew he was in the house."

We headed back toward Rick's house. "Why would somebody take him if they knew him? It's not like he's the kind of kid some childless couple would want to kidnap and raise as their own. I hate to sound rude, but who'd want him?"

"It could be a question of who doesn't want him. Marissa, for one, would have reason to want him out of the way. If he should be proven to be Rick's son, she wouldn't inherit."

I stopped and looked at Fred. "You think Rickie could be..." My sentence trailed off. If I didn't say the word, it wouldn't be real.

"Dead." Fred had no problem expressing himself.

I shuddered. I didn't like the kid, would be perfectly happy never seeing him again for the rest of my life, but I didn't want to think of him dead. "Marissa doesn't fit the description the neighbor's son gave of the kidnapper," I said, trying to make the ugly image go away.

"No, but either of her sons would, and either of them could easily toss Rickie over his shoulder and stroll off with him. Bryan Kollar would fit the description too. Same motive. He has a contract with Marissa to sell him back the flour mill. But if she doesn't inherit, that contract is worthless. If Rickie's not around, she's sure to inherit."

187

I flinched as I remembered my taunt to Bryan the day before about how Rickie might inherit. Was I to blame for Rickie's kidnapping…for his murder?

Fred moved closer to Rick's house and adjusted his earpiece. "This incident could rule out Akin as a suspect since he has nothing to gain by Rickie's disappearance. Too bad. I really don't like him. I'd have enjoyed seeing him go to prison."

"Maybe the kidnapping isn't connected to the attempt on Rick's life, or maybe Akin had a secret desire to be a father to a demon child, and Rickie's still alive somewhere."

Fred arched an eyebrow and ignored me some more while he listened.

A black Cadillac turned into the cul-de-sac, approached the driveway, made a movement to turn in, then straightened as if to drive on past. Marissa. Probably figured the police were there for her. Maybe they were.

She was not getting away so easily. I headed for my sporty little Celica with five on the floor. I could chase her down easily. Not only was my car much sleeker and faster than that tank she was driving, but I doubted that she had my high-speed driving skills. I'd put my speeding tickets up against hers any day.

But just as I reached my car, she stopped, backed up and pulled into the driveway behind me. That was probably a good thing. We had no time to waste. But the thought of a high speed chase had been exciting.

"What's going on?" she asked, sliding out and trying to look nonchalant.

"Rickie's missing," I said.

The door of the house flew open and Grace charged out, shrieking. "What have you done with my son?"

"What?" Marissa looked genuinely confused but I suspected she could mimic any expression she chose.

"You didn't want him to inherit everything, so you kidnapped him!" Grace stopped halfway across the yard and turned to one of the officers who'd followed her outside. "Arrest that woman! She took my Rickie!"

It was possible.

I looked at Fred. He shrugged.

"Where are Clint and Brad?" I asked.

"They're visiting friends," she said evasively.

"Visiting friends? They just got to town. They don't have any friends here. They probably don't have any friends in Crappie Creek or wherever you've been living." My mind filled with images of Rickie bound and gagged somewhere in a dingy motel room while Clint and Brad sat on the stained bed, smoking and playing cards. I grabbed her arm. "Where are they?"

A uniformed officer stepped between Marissa and me. "Can we talk to you inside, ma'am?" he asked Marissa.

She smiled, but it was a twitchy smile. Cops obviously made her nervous. "Of course."

Another patrol car pulled up and stopped. I paid no attention. Just a few more cops. I watched Marissa, studying her expression, trying to decide if the blatant guilt on her face was because she was guilty of all sorts of scams or because she was guilty of something much darker.

Suddenly she stopped, looking toward the street. Her eyes widened, she gasped and her hand flew to her mouth.

Grace shrieked.

I turned to see Trent and Lawson standing beside the latest arrival in the line of cop cars. Lawson was holding the back door open while Rick climbed out.

Chapter Twenty-Two

Fred had been right. The cops had tracked Rick down to his lair. But he wasn't wearing handcuffs. Darn. I'd so hoped he'd be arrested for impersonating a dead man or running from the scene of the crime or something.

"You're not dead?" Marissa blinked a couple of times as if unable to believe her own eyes. "You're alive?" A wide smile slowly spread across her face. "My son's alive!" Probably just me, but I thought the smile was forced and she looked a little disappointed.

Grace recovered from her first moment of shock, ran down the sidewalk and threw herself into his arms. Well, she would have if he'd opened his arms to her. He did sort of put them around her as he tried to balance against the force of her momentum. She looked up at him, her pointy little face a compelling mix of sadness, fear and the new element of hope. "Somebody took our son!"

Rick flinched. "I heard about Rickie." At least he didn't make a scene about not being the boy's father. One point in his very short positive column.

Marissa strode over to him and laid her hand on his cheek. "My son's alive. My prayers have been answered."

191

That was an image I couldn't quite get in focus, Marissa in a church, praying for her dead son's return. Or praying for anything, for that matter. If she wanted something from God, she'd figure out some kind of a scam to run on Him.

"Let's go inside," Trent said, taking Rick's arm and leading him down the sidewalk as Grace held onto his other arm. "Everybody inside," he ordered, though he caught my gaze, frowned and made a very slight movement with his head. Not enough, I decided, to qualify as a shake, a warning not to do something like go inside. No, he was probably just trying to shake off a gnat. I decided to go with that interpretation of the movement.

"Come on," I urged Fred.

"You go ahead. I'm going to drive a few blocks away where I can be sure my phone won't be monitored, then sit in my car and make some calls, see if I can track down a friend who may know something about Kollar."

"Another friend? That makes a total of three, four if you count Jim and Penny as separate friends. Really, Fred, you're pushing the boundaries of my credulity."

"Computers are my friends too."

I could see Fred sitting next to his computer, sipping a glass of wine and conversing with his artificial intelligence buddy. "Okay, I won't ask who your friend is. You think Bryan nabbed Rickie?"

"I don't know, but it's certainly possible. You find out what the police have, and I'll check on Kollar."

"Can I borrow that little eavesdropping device? They may not let me inside. I may have to skulk around the exterior of the house and listen."

Fred reached into his pocket, fumbled, then produced the faux Bluetooth and an individually packaged antibacterial wipe.

I started to lift the device to my ear, but he caught my hand and looked down at the wipe. I rolled my eyes, tore open the package, scrubbed the device and put it in my ear.

"The top button turns it on. Find a quiet place then turn your head in the direction of the sounds you want amplified."

"Where do you get all these cool devices?"

"You can find anything on the Internet."

Maybe I should become better friends with my computer.

I shook my hair so it completely hid my ear and all attachments.

Fred gave an approving nod then turned and strode toward his car.

I followed the crowd inside.

Lawson stopped me at the door. "I'm not sure you should go in there."

I gave him my best withering glare. He didn't wither.

"I'm family," I said. "The missing boy is my nephew."

I glanced at Rick who stood a few feet away. He shook his head firmly and silently mouthed, "He is not."

I knew that, but my lie was small in comparison to the rest of the professional liars gathered around.

193

Lawson shrugged. "If Trent doesn't send you home, I guess it's okay."

Trent was off in a corner talking with one of the uniformed officers. If he said anything to me, I'd tell him Lawson said it was okay for me to be there.

"Can I have your attention, please," Trent said, the commanding tone in his voice causing all conversation to stop. "We have put out an Amber Alert for Rickie Ganyon, and we're doing everything we can to find him. Right now, because you all have a connection to the boy—"

"My sons and I don't," Marissa said.

Trent gave her the evil eye. She sneered at him, but she shut up. "Because all of you have a connection to Rickie, I'd like to talk to each of you, so I'm going to ask that you, Mrs. Malone, have a seat here in the living room and be patient. Mr. Kramer and Miss Ganyon, could you two please come with me to the kitchen?"

Rick and Grace, followed by Lawson and Trent, disappeared into my former kitchen. I strolled casually around to the dining room and sat down at the big oak table which had a polished, pristine surface when I'd last seen it. Now it had several scratch marks and a crayon drawing of a creature that could be a zombie or a vampire or Bryan Kollar having 'roid rage.

I pressed the top button of Fred's device and turned that side of my head toward the common wall that the dining room shared with the kitchen.

"In this sort of situation, we always talk to the parents first." Lawson's voice came through as clearly as if he was sitting next to me.

"Surely you don't think I did anything to hurt my son!" Grace exclaimed.

"I'm not a parent," Rick said.

"Can I join you?" Marissa sank down in a chair next to me.

Damn. I could see the resemblance to Rick. One minute she hated me, next minute she was my best friend. Couldn't get rid of her. She must need something.

I pulled my cell phone from my purse, tucked my hair behind my ear and pointed to the listening device which I hoped she'd mistake for a Bluetooth.

"I'm on the phone," I said.

She glanced down then up again. "No, you're not. The light's not blinking."

"Light's broken." I could hear a conversation going on in the next room, but the conversation in this room kept me from making any sense of it.

"Why did you wait so long to call the police?" Lawson's voice.

"Because..."

"You knew Rick wasn't dead, didn't you?" Marissa accused.

"Trust me, I was as surprised as anybody." I saw no need to tell her when that surprise happened.

"It was all a scam, wasn't it? He faked his own death."

"Good grief, Marissa! You think Rick blew up his car and killed his girlfriend? You think your son committed murder?"

She drummed her long red fingernails on the tabletop and thought for a minute. "I guess not. He's always had a soft heart."

Her definition of a *soft heart* was a lot different from mine.

"The police are picking up Clint and Brad," she said. "Why are they doing that? Why do they want to talk to my boys?"

"I have no idea."

"I can understand why they're questioning Rick. He's pretty tired of Grace claiming that monster child is his son so he'd have reason to get rid of him, but why Clint and Brad? They've never had anything to do with Grace or Rickie."

She could understand why they were questioning Rick? That got my attention. I hadn't given a lot of thought as to why the cops brought Rick to the house. Was he a suspect? Was it possible he'd done something with the kid just to get him out of his life and shut Grace up?

I put my hand over my left ear and strained to hear what was going on in the kitchen.

"...want you to appear in a line-up to see if the boy recognizes you as the man who came here in a van early this morning."

"I told Rick to stay away from that woman. She had her claws out for him from the beginning." Marissa smiled. "Women are attracted to Rick, but you know that, don't you?"

I nodded. Anything to shut her up.

"...can get a court order, but time is critical."

"Of course he'll do it!" Grace was speaking for Rick? I was never allowed to do that.

"A line-up?" Rick repeated. *"Who else besides me?"*

"Your two brothers, you, Bryan Kollar, and Thomas Akin."

"You want to put me in a line-up with the man who tried to kill me?"

Chapter Twenty-Three

Lawson concluded the interview with a request that Rick send Marissa in and that he not leave the building.

"You're up next," I said to the woman who just wouldn't quit jibber-jabbering about Rick and Grace and what the cops could possibly want with her sons.

About that time Rick leaned into the room. "Marissa, the police want to talk to you in the kitchen."

Marissa rose. "And I want to talk to them."

And I wanted to hear that conversation.

Of course Rick sat down at the table as soon as his mother left. "Lindsay, they want to put me in a line-up."

"You'll live. They're just going to look at you, not execute you. Go away."

He leaned across the table toward me. "A line-up with Thomas Akin! He's probably the one who blew up my car and tried to kill me! They can't put me in the same room with him!"

True to his nature, Rick was concerned with what might happen to him, not the fact that a woman had actually died in the explosion or that a kid was missing. "You'll be in a police station, surrounded by cops. Be quiet or *I'll* kill you."

"The boys were visiting friends last night," I heard Marissa say.

Grace walked into the room and sat down next to Rick.

I glared at both of them. "I don't remember sending out an invitation saying the party's in here."

"I can't stand to think something bad has happened to our son," Grace said, trying to take Rick's arm. He pulled away from her.

"Your boy's going to be fine," Rick assured her. "He's just wandered off. Boys do that." He didn't look like he believed his own words. He didn't look like he cared either.

"A line-up?" I didn't need the device to hear Marissa's loud exclamation. It came quite clearly through the wall. *"You are not putting my boys in a line-up like they were common criminals!"*

Grace and Rick both grinned.

"I'm not saying another word without my attorney! This conversation is over!"

Marissa stormed out of the kitchen into the living room. "Get out!" she shouted, apparently addressing the two uniformed officers who remained in the house and probably Rick, Grace and me. "All of you, get out!"

Rick stood and walked over to her. "Marissa, this is my house. You can't order people to leave."

She glared at him. "Then you do it!"

Trent and Lawson emerged from the kitchen. "Rick," Lawson said, "we'd like to ask you to come down to the station with us now. Your brothers and Thomas Akin have been located and are on their way. We're still trying to find Bryan Kollar, but we need to move with urgency on this line-up so we'll proceed without him if we have to. Miss Ganyon, please remain here in case your son returns."

Rick scowled and Grace nodded.

Everyone left except Grace, Marissa and me.

Marissa joined us at the table.

"Detective Lawson didn't say you had to stay," I pointed out.

"He didn't say you had to either," she snapped.

"My name's on the title to this house." I really didn't want to be there, but I needed to wait for Fred. Besides, I wasn't about to let Marissa run me off.

"So is my son's name."

I shrugged. "I guess that makes us one big, happy family, and we can all hang out here in perfect harmony as soon as I buy everybody a Coke."

Marissa scowled. "You've really got a sarcastic mouth on you."

I smiled. "Thank you."

Grace burst into tears. "How can you two argue when my son may be lying dead in some dark alley?"

"Whether or not we argue isn't going to make your son any less dead," Marissa said.

That comment didn't improve Grace's sobbing.

I took a packet of tissues from my purse and handed them to her. "It's going to be okay. The police are on it. They know what they're doing. They've done this before." I didn't like the woman, but I did feel sorry for her.

"If they knew what they were doing," Marissa said, "they wouldn't be dragging my sons in for a line-up to see if that kid next door can identify one of them! I told them they can't do that without my permission!"

"Actually, I'm pretty sure they can. I'm going to take a wild guess and say that your sons are both over the age of eighteen, so the cops don't need your permission to talk to them."

"I'm still their mother!"

"And a fine job you've done of that. What are you worried the police are going to find out? Where were your sons last night? I hope this time they didn't choose another undercover cop to sell themselves to. After meeting you, I understand why Rick's so messed up."

She arched a perfect eyebrow. "If you'd been any kind of a wife, you'd have been able to keep him."

"Like you kept their father?"

"Stop it, both of you!" Grace shouted. Tears streamed down her face.

"Shut up, you sniveling little bitch," Marissa snarled.

I didn't like Grace, but I didn't like Marissa more. "I think you need to leave," I said.

"And I think I need to stay right here."

I stood and picked up one of the heavy brass candlesticks that sat in the middle of the table. "Get out," I said. "Now."

"Are you threatening me?" She rose too.

I laughed. "How clever you are to figure that out!"

We did a little posturing and puffing out our chests, my mother-in-law and I. She had me on the puffing out chests thing, but I beat her on the posturing since I'm taller. Apparently meaner too since she gave first.

"My son will hear about this!" She turned and stormed out of the room.

"Tell him! What's he going to do? Divorce me?" I shouted at her departing back.

Grace gave a weak smile. "Thank you."

I flopped back down into my chair. "Don't thank me. I've been wanting to run that woman off since the first time I met her."

"She's the reason me and Rick broke up. We were getting along just fine until I got pregnant, and then she convinced him the baby wasn't his. It is his baby. I wasn't cheating on him. I loved him."

I shifted in my chair. A part of me wanted to tell her that Marissa and Rick knew the baby wasn't his because he'd had a vasectomy, but Rick should be the one to tell her that. Besides, I wasn't a hundred percent sure he really had. He'd sounded sincere when he told me, but it wouldn't be the first time Rick had lied, always with the utmost sincerity.

"It's going to be all right." I uttered the inane phrase with as much confidence as I could muster. I had no idea if it was going to be all right, if the cops would ever find Rickie and if he'd be alive or dead when they did.

కావ

Grace was in the midst of telling me stories about how cute, darling and destructive Rickie had always been when Fred came in.

"Lindsay, we need to leave," he said, his voice pulling me from my Grace-induced stupor.

I wanted nothing more than to get away from the boring litany of Rickie's charming misdeeds, but I felt guilty about leaving Grace alone.

"We'll have to wait until Rick gets back," I said, inclining my head toward Grace.

"I'll be fine." She lifted a crumpled tissue to blot the fresh flow of tears.

Fred checked his watch and heaved a huge sigh. "We can wait a few minutes. Rick should be here soon."

"They already did the line-up?"

"They do things fast in a possible child abduction."

Grace looked up from her tissue. "Did they find out anything about who took Rickie?"

Fred shook his head. "The kid couldn't identify anybody. Said it was too dark, and he wasn't paying attention. The guy had something on his head, probably a ski mask, so he didn't see a face. As far as general body build, it could have been any of the men." He looked directly at me. "They can't find Bryan Kollar. We can wait for up to fifteen minutes if..." He paused and appeared to be in pain. Excruciating pain. "If you drive."

I'm sure my chin dropped to the tabletop. It would have gone all the way to the floor if I'd been standing. "You're going to ride with me?"

"I don't have any choice. We can't be late for this appointment."

I smiled and leaned back, clasping my hands behind my head. "This day will go down in history."

"Only if we survive."

Rick was there in ten minutes. As soon as he came in the door, Grace ran to him, her tears starting again. He gave me a helpless look.

"You're up," I said to him as Fred and I headed for the door. "Grace has nowhere to go, and she shouldn't be left alone."

Rick tried to fend off Grace. "I can't stay here. I have to hide. Akin threatened me right there in the police station!"

"Was he the one who took our son?" Grace asked.

"I don't know. Maybe." Rick moved over to the window and looked out. "There he is! He followed me home! He's going to kill me!"

Fred walked over to the window. "That big guy who looks like a basset hound?"

Rick turned away and drew a shaky hand across his upper lip, wiping away the perspiration. "That's him. What's he doing?"

"Nothing. Getting out of his car." Fred turned back to Rick. "I'll make you a deal. You stay here with Grace, and I'll get rid of Akin."

Rick looked doubtful.

Fred checked his watch. "We're in a hurry. You have eight seconds to make a decision."

"Yeah, sure, okay."

Fred strolled outside. I watched through the window as he sauntered up to the oaf coming down the sidewalk. The man did, indeed, look like a sad old basset hound. I hadn't seen a picture of Julia, but I assumed she was attractive or Rick wouldn't have bothered with her. This creep must have money.

The two men met halfway down the walk. Fred was as tall as Akin, but Akin outweighed him by a good fifty pounds. It was going to be really funny when Fred took him down with a well-aimed kick. I smiled as I watched the confrontation.

Fred said something quietly, something I couldn't hear. Darn.

"I want that little pipsqueak to look me in the eye and admit to me that he slept with my wife!" Akin bellowed. "I'm not going to hurt him, but I could, and there's not a jury in the country that would convict me! He took my property!"

Now! I thought. *Take him down now!*

Fred spoke quietly again.

Akin paled, glared at the house then turned around and walked rapidly back to his car, got in and drove away.

That was disappointing.

Fred came back inside. "Ready, Lindsay?"

"What did you say to him?" Rick asked, his expression a blend of awe and shock.

"I told him I was going to kill you myself, and if he got in my way, I'd kill him too. Let's go, Lindsay."

Rick opened his mouth as if to speak but no words came out.

I walked out the door leaving Grace in the not-so-capable hands of her former lover.

"Is that really what you said to Akin?" I asked as we hurried to Fred's car.

"In a way."

He started to get in the driver's side.

I stopped him. "We're late. I'm driving. Remember?"

He looked at my car then at his. His face contorted as if he was making a life or death decision. "If we take your car, you have to drive both ways."

"Or I drive one way and you walk back."

He drew in a deep breath, crossed himself and handed me the keys to his car.

I stood for a moment in complete shock. "I get to drive your car?"

"Get in before I change my mind."

"That cross thing, I didn't know you were Catholic," I said, sliding in the car while Fred held the door.

"I wasn't until I started thinking about riding with you."

And people say I'm sarcastic.

"Get in, hold on and don't scream. It's so distracting when people scream while I'm driving."

Chapter Twenty-Four

Fred didn't scream, but he did gasp a few times as we drove across town to an office building in a strip mall in Lee's Summit, a quiet suburb southeast of Kansas City.

"Expert Enterprises?" I read the sign printed in black block letters on the window. "What does this company do?"

Fred unfolded himself from the car. "Expert stuff." He extended a hand for the car keys.

Darn. I'd hoped he might forget. His Mercedes, big and bulky as it was, had a surprising amount of pep to it. Fred probably tinkered with the engine. Besides, watching him almost have a heart attack every time I slid around a corner or cut in front of another car with inches to spare was fun.

We entered through the glass door, and a perfectly groomed brunette woman sitting behind the desk looked up and smiled. "May I help you?"

"Fred Sommers to see Donato Orsini."

With all the vowels in the man's name and the generic company name, I was suspicious about what kind of place we'd come to. Kansas City used to have a huge mob presence. They didn't make the headlines much anymore, but I felt sure there were still some of them around.

An inner door burst open and a short, dark man with gray hair and a wide grin stepped out. "Fred Sommers!" He came over to Fred and the two men embraced. Fred had to lean down about a foot. The man punched Fred's arm. "Long time no see! Come on in. How you doing? Bring us some coffee, Teresa, and hold my calls. Me and Fred got a lot of catching up to do."

He led us into his sedate, immaculate office, an office that matched the man's dark silk suit but seemed at odds with the rough-hewn man himself. "This your woman?"

"This is my associate, Lindsey Powell. Lindsay, an old friend, Donato Orsini."

"Nice to meet you, Mr. Orsini." I extended a hand across the desk.

He grasped my hand in both of his. "Please, I'm Donato. I'm not old enough to be Mr. Orsini. Nice to meet you, Lindsay." He looked at Fred and winked. "Associate, eh? Whatever you say, buddy." He winked again and finally released my hand. "Sit, sit."

We sat in the two client chairs. The place looked like a made-for-TV version of an office. Desk, chairs and file cabinet, all the right furnishings. But the only items on the polished walnut surface of his desk were a telephone, a wooden box and a crystal ashtray. What sort of business was conducted in this room, and what were we doing there?

Donato opened the wooden box, took out a cigar and extended it to Fred.

Fred frowned. "Donato, haven't you read the reports on smoking? Are you suicidal?"

I wondered if Fred was suicidal, asking a question like that of the man in front of us.

Donato cracked up laughing. "I forgot how much you hate smoke," he said, putting his own cigar back into the box. Whatever business the man was in, I couldn't fault his manners.

He leaned back in his leather desk chair and folded his hands over his comfortably rounded stomach. "So what have you been up to the last few years? You're looking good, my man."

"I'm retired. How about you?"

Donato waved an arm around the office. "Retired and got a legitimate business going."

"I'll keep you in mind if I need any experts." Fred smiled.

Donato chuckled and winked. "You do that. I got the experts, all right."

Teresa appeared carrying a tray with three mugs of steaming coffee, all imprinted with the Italian flag and *Italians rule.*

I tried to keep my hand from shaking as I took one of the mugs. I don't drink coffee, but I wasn't about to refuse that cup.

Was Fred retired from the mob?

Teresa set three coasters on the desk and left.

Fred sipped his coffee. "Excellent." He placed his cup squarely on one of the coasters. "I'm not in the market for an expert today, but I could use some information."

"Got plenty of that too."

"Bryan Kollar. I understand you know him."

Donato nodded. "The Kollar kid. He's done all right for himself."

"What can you tell me about him?"

"Bennie Fanello's kid."

"I thought his parents were teachers," I blurted then immediately regretted drawing attention to myself.

Donato looked at me. "The people that adopted him, yeah, they're teachers. But he's Bennie's kid, all right. Looks just like him. Remember, they used to call him Bennie the Beautiful, but only behind his back!"

Fred nodded. "I remember."

"One of Bennie's bimbos got pregnant and wanted him to leave the missus and marry her. That wasn't happening, of course, so she gave the baby away. Probably a good thing. The Kollars, they're good people. The girlfriend, not so much." He took a sip of his coffee.

I held onto my cup, uncertain if it would be an insult if I set it on his desk untasted, and unwilling to find out.

Donato noticed. "You don't like the coffee?"

"She's a Coke drinker."

"Why didn't you say so? Teresa!" he bellowed. "Go down the street and get Fred's woman some Coke!"

"No," I protested. "I'm fine, really." I set the cooling cup of coffee on one of the coasters.

"She's trying to quit," Fred said.

Donato shrugged. "Never mind, Teresa!"

"About Bryan Kollar?" Fred prompted.

"Anyway, Bennie didn't know what happened to the kid. Probably didn't give it much thought, you know? But then one day one of his people comes in from selling some stuff to the college kids and says he's seen a boy looks like Bennie. Bennie checked into the records and found out it was his son."

Checked into the records? He made it sound so easy, like the easy way Fred did things. My suspicions about Fred's past grew.

"You're not going to believe it," Donato continued, "but that kid was skin and bones when Bennie found him. He was mixed up with a bunch of losers, experimenting with drugs. Bennie wanted to do the right thing by the boy. He got him off drugs and into body building, and right away..." Donato spread his arms. "Overnight that kid turned into the man you see on television today."

"Off drugs?" I asked. "He did all that without steroids?"

Donato shrugged. "Got him off the bad stuff. That kid was a skeleton. He needed all the help he could get."

"Bennie give him the money for his first gym?" Fred asked.

"Yeah, sure. It was a business deal. Bennie gave him the money, and Kollar gave him a percentage of his business."

"What about the Kollars' sporting goods store?"

"That was a separate deal. Kollar wanted to do that for his folks, so Bennie made him a personal loan. He paid back every penny with interest."

"Was Bryan ever an employee?"

Donato shook his head. "Nah. He runs his gyms and pays his dues. Bennie didn't want him to get involved. Didn't want his wife to know he was helping his son by another woman, either."

211

We'd learned that Bryan did steroids and was in bed with the mob, which was pretty interesting, but it didn't prove Bryan tried to kill Rick, didn't give him a motive.

I summoned up my courage. "Mr. Orsini...Donato...do you know of any reason Bryan Kollar would be unwilling to part with his family's old flour mill out north of town?" I asked.

Donato scratched his nose and looked at me then at Fred. "You trust her?"

"With my life."

Considering he'd just ridden with me across town, that was no idle remark.

"That old flour mill, it hadn't been used by the Kollar family in over fifty years. The kid sort of leased it to Bennie back in the day. Let him hide a few bodies there."

"A few?" I choked on the words.

"A hundred, two hundred. I don't think anybody kept track of them on a spreadsheet." He laughed at his own joke.

Chapter Twenty-Five

"Call me. Let's go get some dinner sometime. Don't be such a stranger," Donato said as we walked through the front office of Expert Enterprises.

"I will," Fred promised.

"You too, associate."

"You bet," I said.

"Coke, no coffee." He winked. "Next time."

We got in the car, and Fred began his slow crawl across town. Now that I knew how much power that car had, his insistence on observing the speed limit really baffled me. And irritated me. It wasn't like he didn't break the law in plenty of other ways.

"Were you a member of the mob?" I asked.

He frowned. "No, of course I wasn't."

"Then how do you know this guy?"

"I know a lot of people. Comes in handy. Now we have a motive for Kollar wanting to get the flour mill back. He may not have known what Rick wanted to do with the property, but he couldn't take any chances."

"Which gives him a motive for killing Rick when Rick refused to sell it to him. It also gives him a reason to want Rickie out of the way especially now that he knows about the plans for a shopping center. As long as Marissa inherited, he could get the

213

property back, but Grace was going to hang onto everything for her son. So now Rickie's missing, and Bryan couldn't be found for the line-up. That does look pretty suspicious."

Fred nodded. His expression was grim. Fred doesn't often do grim. When he does, I know things have become serious. "There's probably no chance the boy's still alive," he said, "but on the slim chance he is, we need to find Kollar as soon as we can."

I swallowed around the huge lump that suddenly rose in my throat. "You're right. Just taking Rickie wouldn't accomplish anything. He needs to get rid of him. You think he killed him?" My last words came out barely above a whisper. I couldn't stand the awful child, but I couldn't stand to think of him being murdered either.

"Probably. We won't know until we find Kollar."

"The cops already looked for him to get him in the line-up. I wonder if they checked the old flour mill."

"Did you say anything to Trent about that deal?"

"No, I don't think so. There's been so much else to talk about...Marissa and the boys, Rickie, Rick's reincarnation."

"Then there's no reason they would go out there. The place was never in Bryan's name." Fred made an abrupt turn around the corner. Well, abrupt for him. For me it would have been a lazy amble. "Since it's been a body dump site before, it would be the logical place for him to hide a body. You might want to call Trent and give him a heads up."

I took my cell phone out of my purse and hit speed dial for Trent's cell. To my amazement, he actually answered.

"Where are you?" I asked.

"At the courthouse trying to convince a judge to sign off on a search warrant for Bryan Kollar's condo." He sighed. "Everybody agrees it's significant that we can't find the guy right after Rickie disappears and the news hits all the local television stations that Rick's still alive, but nobody seems to think it's enough to justify a search warrant."

"The news is out that Rick's still alive? When did that happen?"

"Shortly after we pulled him out of hiding today to question him about Rickie's disappearance. We don't seem to have any secrets from the media."

I turned to Fred. "Bryan may know that Rick's still alive."

"Which means Rick may not be alive much longer."

"Who are you talking to?" Trent asked.

"I'm talking to Fred." I told Trent our theory about Bryan's possible involvement in Rickie's kidnapping and the attempt on Rick's life. "We're on our way to the old Kollar Flour Mill out north. When you were trying to find him for the line-up, did you check there?"

"No, we had no reason to. We went to his condo, but he didn't answer, then we went to all seven of his gyms. Everybody said they hadn't seen him today, but everybody lies."

I couldn't argue with that since I'd done my share of lying lately. But always in a good cause.

"If he's the one who took Rickie, we think he might go out to the flour mill because…"

I looked at Fred. He didn't move his eyes from the road, but he shook his head firmly. Yeah, we didn't want to be squealing on the mob.

"Because why?" Trent asked.

"Because…that's the only place you haven't looked. Just trust me on this one, okay? And you don't need a search warrant to go there because Rick owns it and can give you permission. If he's still alive."

I can't say I felt happy and excited at the thought that I had another chance at getting rid of Rick. But I can't say I didn't either.

"Great," Trent said. "I get to talk to your husband again and try to keep him from getting killed."

"Maybe not. Kollar may have him too."

"Lawson and I will go by his place and pick him up if he's still there, put him in protective custody and get his permission to search the flour mill, then head out there. You and Fred should go back home."

"Excuse me? This was our idea!"

"Lindsay, this is a police matter. If Kollar is the one who murdered Julia and tried to murder Rick, and if he did grab Rickie, this is going to be dangerous."

"Dangerous? You think it wasn't dangerous when that crazy woman broke into my house and tried to kill me or when Paula's crazy ex poisoned me? I think I can handle a little danger."

"Lindsay, please. Do as I ask just this once. If we do find Rickie, we don't need civilians around to worry about."

"Okay." I often use that word as a contraction for the much longer phrase, *It's okay if that's what you want to think, and I'm not going to argue with you, but I'm going to do as I please.* I used to worry that people would figure it out after the twentieth or thirtieth time, but they haven't so far.

I said good-bye to Trent and put my phone back in my purse.

Fred grinned. "I can't believe he still falls for your *okay* routine."

Well, nobody except Fred figured it out. Fred's psychic and has super powers, so he doesn't count.

❧⚜❧

In spite of Fred's driving, we arrived at the flour mill before Trent. Probably because he had to stop by Rick's house and, maybe, phone in a homicide report when he found Rick's body. Yeah, I'm a total optimist.

However, someone was at the mill. An old black minivan sat in the overgrown parking lot. Fred pulled in behind it and we got out. The place felt eerily deserted.

We started toward the building, crunched through the weeds, probably walking over the graves of several unfortunate souls who got on the wrong side of Bennie the Beautiful.

The door that had previously hung askew on one hinge now lay in the dirt. Before we even stepped inside, I could smell gunpowder residue. We walked cautiously through the open door. Well, I walked cautiously. Fred strode in as if he had an engraved invitation.

It had been a mess before, but now even that mess was a mess. The dust, dirt, straw and spider webs had been disturbed as if WWE had held a tag team wrestling match there. The ladder leading up to the loft had several more broken rungs.

Fred walked over to the wall. "Bullet holes."

"New ones? Maybe they were left over from a mob event years ago," I said hopefully.

"Yes, new ones. Several of them."

I looked around the room. "I don't see any blood, at least not down here."

I went over to the ladder. Several of the breaks were fresh. "Rickie?" I called. "Are you up there?" *Are you up there alive?* I couldn't see him through any of the holes in the ceiling, but there were a few solid spots left.

Fred took my arm. "Don't even think about going up there. Let's go outside. We'll find another way."

We went out the door and started around the building. I saw a broken window on the second floor but no way to get up there. However, the ground beneath the window showed signs of someone having been there recently. The weeds were crushed as if someone had jumped from a great height. I stooped to examine the ground closer.

"Look." Fred's voice drew my attention to a mound of dirt and debris several feet closer to the back of the building.

We walked over and found that the debris was pieces of bones.

The property directly behind the building had several of those mounds.

"He was trying to dig a grave for Rickie, but everywhere he dug, he found another body," Fred said quietly.

A shot exploded from somewhere in the dense forest of trees and brush.

Chapter Twenty-Six

"Was that what I think it was?"

Fred nodded. "If you think it was a gun shot, then it was what you think."

"I guess that's a good sign. If he's shooting at Rickie, that surely means he hasn't killed him yet, right?"

"Brilliant deduction. I think it came from that direction."

We started in the direction Fred pointed, but the sound of a car arriving stopped us.

"It's probably Trent," I said. I hoped it was Trent.

We hurried back around the building and saw Trent and Lawson getting out of his car. Lawson opened the back door to let two passengers out.

Rick and Grace.

Rick was still alive and safe. No point in my buying a lottery ticket with that kind of luck.

"Lindsay?" Trent looked a little irritated. Okay, a lot irritated. "I thought you were going home."

"Eventually I am. Fred found bullet holes inside, and it looks like Rickie escaped. You need our help finding him. There's a lot of ground to cover out there."

"Rickie escaped? He's okay?" Grace exclaimed, clasping her hands and starting toward me. Lawson restrained her.

"We've got officers coming in to help search. Fred, please take her home."

"Okay."

Well, bless his heart. Fred had learned something from me.

Another shot came from the same direction as the first.

Grace gasped. Rick flinched and shoved his hands into his pockets.

"Stay here, Lindsay." Fred loped off in the direction of the shots.

I followed. He knew I would. He was just trying to appease Trent.

"Lindsay!" Trent shouted.

"Okay!" I called over my shoulder.

"Damn it, Lindsay! Come back here!"

If he kept talking like that, we'd never make it to the bedroom. I don't like being ordered around.

Fred and I crashed into the dense growth of trees, bushes and weeds.

"BRYAN KOLLAR," Lawson's voice boomed from behind us, magically amplified by their bullhorn. "WE KNOW YOU'RE OUT THERE. WE HAVE A SWAT TEAM COMING IN. YOU NEED TO RETURN TO THE BUILDING."

I tripped over a rock.

No, I tripped over a skull.

"You okay?" Fred asked.

"Not really. Let's go."

"Watch where you're stepping."

"Actually, I think I'd rather not see where I'm stepping."

"BRYAN, PLEASE BRING BACK MY BABY BOY." Grace's amplified nasal tones were painful to the ear. "PLEASE DON'T HURT HIM."

"Mama!"

Rickie!

Fred took a left turn, moving faster on foot than when he drives. I hurried to keep up.

Someone screamed.

Ahead I could see Bryan Kollar's famous butt as he bent forward, clutching his groin and groaning.

A small figure sprinted away, darting around the trees and bushes.

"Rickie! Stop!" I called.

Fred charged toward Kollar, but the man sprinted away. He had apparently recovered from whatever injury Rickie had inflicted on him, and he was in good physical shape. Fred was tall and lanky, a little on the thin side, but, as far as I could tell, made of steel. Kollar was in trouble.

Crashing sounds came from behind us. Probably the cops. To be honest, I wouldn't mind seeing them at that point.

"Rickie!" Grace's voice, but she was too small to make that much noise thrashing around. Had to be some cops back there too.

Another shot rang out. I couldn't tell if it came from in front of us or behind us. Could be Kollar shooting at Rickie or at Fred and me or it could be Trent shooting at Kollar...or Trent shooting at me for ignoring his orders.

I had no idea who was where or what direction we were headed, but I followed Fred.

"Rickie! Baby, come to Mama!" Grace was doing a pretty good job of following us.

Police sirens screamed, moving closer then stopping.

"BRYAN KOLLAR, THE SWAT TEAM IS HERE, AND WE'RE COMING IN AFTER YOU." Lawson on the bullhorn again.

A small form darted out of the bushes. A larger form shot out, made a flying tackle and grabbed the kid only a few feet away from us.

"Give it up, Kollar," Fred ordered.

Bryan rolled expertly to his feet with one arm wrapped around Rickie's neck, the other holding a gun to the boy's head. Bryan didn't look so beautiful anymore. Leaves and twigs intertwined among his once perfect locks of hair. His clothes were torn and dirty, and his face and arms were covered in scratches. His eyes were wild.

"Rickie!" Grace struggled in. One of her heels had broken, but she was still coming, heading straight for her son.

"I won't miss from this distance!" Bryan threatened.

I grabbed Grace around the waist and stopped her progress.

Fred eased closer to Bryan. Still about ten feet away, too far to land a kick. "You having trouble hitting your target, Bryan? Never shot a gun before? Bennie made it look easy, but it isn't, is it?"

223

Bryan licked his lips, his eyes darting around as if for answers to what had become a no-win situation for him.

Fred moved a few inches nearer. "You don't really want to do this, buddy. He's just a little kid."

Fred could take people out with a well-aimed kick. Trent had a nifty gun that took people out from a long ways away. I had an attack cat who was locked in my house twenty miles away. I was at a distinct disadvantage, so I just did my best to hang onto Grace who was a lot stronger than she looked and very determined to get to her son.

"My baby!" Grace shrieked.

"He's a monster!" Bryan flinched as Rickie continued to struggle, kicking against his legs and trying to bite his arm. "This kid is not normal! I left him drugged to the gills, lying on the floor. But I couldn't find any place to dig a…to dig a place to put him." He blinked as sweat ran down his forehead and into his eyes. "Those people, my father, they put them everywhere!"

"But you're not like those people." A half step closer. "That man's not really your father. Walter Kollar's your father. He had nothing to do with all this."

Kollar bit his lip and pressed the gun harder against Rickie's head. The boy continued his efforts to get away. "I gave him enough drugs to take down an elephant, but when I got back inside, he was wide awake. Look at me! Look at what this brat did to me! I'm bleeding and he kicked me in the balls and my clothes are ruined! He's nothing but a snotty-nosed kid, and I'm Bryan Kollar, but look at what he did to me!"

"Kollar! Let the boy go!" Trent came up with a gun, a big gun, pointed directly at Bryan Kollar.

"Hey! What are you doing?" Rick rushed forward. Fred held out an arm to stop him.

Bryan's face went even paler and his grip on Rickie slackened, the gun pressed less tightly to his head. "What are you doing here? I killed you!"

Guess Bryan hadn't heard the news about Rick's miraculous return from the dead.

"This is all your fault!" He turned loose of Rickie and aimed the gun directly at Rick. "If you would've sold me back this property, none of this would have happened!"

Trent's gun exploded just as Fred launched himself at Bryan.

For an instant I was afraid Fred might have been shot, but immediately blood blossomed from one of Bryan's shoulders just as Fred's heel connected with his chin and the man dropped to the ground.

Grace broke free of my grip and ran to her son, enfolding him in her arms.

Trent strode over to Bryan who lay on the ground cursing Rick and Rickie and Marissa and me and the rock under his head and the world in general. Trent yanked him to his feet and clapped handcuffs on him.

Fred stood to the side. Trent turned to him and smiled. "Where did that come from?"

Fred shrugged. "I know a little karate."

Kollar snarled.

Grace pulled Rick into a group hug. "You tried to save our son!"

Rick looked helpless.

I smiled.

Chapter Twenty-Seven

I made it through work the next day in spite of being stressed, scratched from the weeds and brush, and generally freaked out. But the people need their chocolate.

My special that day was Cookie Dough Cheesecake Bars. Yes, I know I'd served it only a few days before, but this one was for me. I needed a special treat.

I kept my cell phone on the counter, waiting to hear more news about Bryan's arrest, Rickie's recovery and Rick's relatives. I was pleased that none of them showed up at my restaurant. A couple of Cokes, a lot of chocolate, no appearances from Rick's relatives or his would-be killer, and my stress level was going down measurably. I wasn't sure Rick would follow through on his promise to Fred to sign the divorce papers since the cops had found him anyway, but even if he didn't, that situation was no worse than it had been…and maybe he would keep his word for once.

"Why don't you take off early?" Paula suggested as the last customer walked out the door and she locked up behind him. "I can clean up."

"I took off early yesterday and left you to clean, and I have to say, I'd rather have been here scraping crumbs off dirty plates."

She smiled as she picked up the dishes from the last table. "So today you stay here and clean, and I'll go trip over a few skulls and chase after a murderer."

I dipped my cloth in bleach water and wiped the counter. "That sounds like a deal."

Finally my cell phone rang…Trent. We'd spoken briefly last night after the big take-down, but only to assure each other we were okay. I thought it probably wasn't the best time to bring up the subject again of how much I needed a gun, and he was smart enough not to bring up the subject again of how I'd disobeyed his orders and ended up in the middle of a takedown.

"Hey, big cop, want a cookie?" I said in greeting.

"Yeah, I do." I could hear the smile in his voice. "Maybe we could grab a burger tonight and talk about those cookies."

"Works for me." I could only hope my newly-incarnated estranged husband wouldn't show up. "How's Bryan Kollar? Did he get out on bail yet?"

"Not yet, and I'm not sure he will. We've found over a hundred bodies on the grounds of that flour mill, and even though he claims he had nothing to do with their murders, he knew they were there. He did admit to killing Thomas Akin's wife, but he's claiming that was an accident. Says he didn't know she'd be in that car, and she wouldn't have been in that car if she wasn't cheating on her husband, so it's not his fault."

"Ah, the old *not my fault* defense. He said yesterday it was all Rick's fault he tried to kill him and Rickie, that Rick could have sold him back the property and avoided the whole mess."

"Sad thing is, I think he really believes it. If he'd never met his real father, that gangster, and been influenced by the man's values, he might have turned out to be a different person."

"Did Bennie teach him how to make the bomb he used on Rick's car?"

"No, he said he got that off the Internet, and he hadn't meant for it to be quite so powerful. The directions must have been wrong. Again, not his fault."

"I feel sorry for his parents. The ones who raised him, I mean. They seem like nice people."

"They're standing by him, but they're pretty upset. They want him to own up to what he did and take his punishment. However, he's hired a team of high powered lawyers and keeps protesting that none of it was his fault. We'll see what happens. I imagine he'll be spending at least a few years behind bars. He should have plenty of time in prison to work out and stay in shape."

"You caught the bad guy and made the streets of Pleasant Grove a safer place. I'll have an appropriate reward waiting for you tonight."

He laughed softly. "Just seeing you will be enough reward. You know, when I order you to do something, I'm not trying to push you around. I just worry about you. You're a little bull-headed about putting yourself in dangerous situations."

"I don't take orders well. Look at it this way. If I made every chocolate recipe the way it's already been written, I'd be making mediocre chocolate. I look at the directions and decide how I can make it better. That's what I do when you order me to do something. I think about it, but I make my own decision."

He was quiet for a few seconds. "I'll see you tonight."

A wise man. He knew when to give up.

☙❧

Henry met me at the door, purred loudly, gave me a couple of head butts, allowed me to stroke him once, then led me back to the kitchen to show me his empty food bowl. Life was getting back to normal. The only part of that I wasn't crazy about was the part where I was still legally entangled with Rick. I had called him and, no big surprise, he said he didn't remember making any deal with Fred about signing any papers.

I followed Henry to the kitchen and filled his bowl. "No more strange people in the house," I promised him. He didn't stop eating, but he did switch his tail as if in acknowledgment and approval. "Trent's coming over tonight, but you like him." Another tail switch.

I pulled out a chair from the table and sat. "However, it's probably still going to be just you and me tonight. As long as I'm legally bound to that jerk, Trent's very likely going to stick to his antiquated moral code." Though I complained about Trent's outdated belief, I kind of liked it. The idea, that is, not the reality that came along with the idea.

A knock sounded on my front door, and my heart sank. Had Rick kicked out his relatives and they'd come back to my house?

Henry lifted his head as if testing the air for...whatever cats test the air for. Scents? Feelings? Auras? He went calmly back to eating, unalarmed, so I felt safe in going to answer my front door.

Fred, looking quite smug and pleased with himself, stood on my porch with a folder in his hand. "We're going over to see Rick, and he's going to make you a very happy woman."

"You have anthrax in that folder, and he's going to sniff some of it?"

Fred rolled his eyes. "You need to get over that blood-thirsty tendency."

"I was doing fine until Rick showed up in my shower."

"Get your purse and let's go."

"Trent's coming over. How long will this take?"

"Not long if you'll get a move on."

"Let me tell Henry we're leaving and see if he wants to go out now or finish eating first."

"You act like that cat can understand you."

"That would be because he does." Fred's smart, but he still had a lot to learn about cats. "Are we taking my car or yours?"

"Mine."

"Can I drive?"

"Of course not."

Henry elected to go out before we left and finish dinner later. I grabbed my purse and we set off for Rick's house.

"Is he expecting us?" I asked as Fred drove slowly down the street.

"I didn't want to ruin the surprise."

"Are you sure he's home?"

"Yes."

❧❧

The shiny rental Cadillac and the pitiful battered Ford both sat in Rick's driveway when we pulled up to his house. I assumed his new car was inside the garage. He'd managed to get the cars out of his house but not the relatives.

Marissa answered the door. She studied us for a moment then decided to go with manners. "Come in," she said with a tight smile, stepping back and holding the door open to allow us entrance. "We're having a barbecue to celebrate the safe return of my son and Grace's son. You're welcome to join us."

"Thank you." Fred stepped inside, and I followed.

The place still looked like a disaster area. Whatever happened on this visit, I would always recall with delight seeing Rick in this setting.

Marissa directed us through the kitchen and out to the back yard where Rick, Brad and Clint were presiding over a grill covered in hot dogs and hamburgers.

Rick looked up as we came out the patio door. Charcoal streaked one cheek and his shirt, and he didn't look happy. Rickie seemed permanently attached to his side.

Brad and Clint didn't look happy either. Grace, sitting in one of the patio chairs with a glass of wine in her hand, looked positively ecstatic. "It's your

Aunt Lindsay," she said. Rickie detached himself from Rick and ran over to me.

I was pleased Bryan Kollar had failed in his plan to kill the kid, but that was as far as my good will went. I stood stiffly while he wrapped his thin arms around me. "Aunt Lindsay!"

"He's having such a good time getting to know his uncles and his grandmother and, of course, his daddy." Grace sipped her wine and beamed.

"I am not his grandmother," Marissa said through gritted teeth, moving around to take a seat across the patio from Grace and retrieving her own glass of wine from a nearby table. "Clint and Brad are not his uncles, and Rick is not his father."

"Actually," Fred said, opening his folder and taking out a set of stapled papers featuring graphs and text, "when it comes to Rickie Ganyon, Rick is his father, you are his grandmother, and Clint and Brad are his uncles."

For a moment nobody moved or spoke. The birds even stopped singing and the leaves stopped moving in the trees. Well, that's how it seemed.

"I told you!" Grace jumped to her feet and ran to throw her arms around Rick.

He stood frozen in place, his hamburger flipper halfway under a patty. "But," he protested softly, "that's not possible.

Fred walked over and handed him the papers. "Not all vasectomies are successful."

"Vasectomy?" Grace exclaimed.

Marissa stepped up and snatched the papers from Fred. "Yes, he had a vasectomy. I saw to it." She studied the papers then ripped them in two. Before

233

she could tear them another time, Rick dropped his hamburger turner and grabbed them from her.

"How competent was this doctor you used, Marissa?" I asked. I have to confess, I was enjoying the scene. "How many vasectomies had he done? What was his specialty? Did he normally take out tonsils?"

"Well…" Marissa's smile faltered, and her hands fell to her sides. "He didn't exactly graduate from medical school, but he had the necessary training."

"Apparently not." I looked around at Clint and Brad to see how they were taking the news. They had gone quite pale.

"I couldn't afford a real doctor after your father left me," she said defensively.

Ah, we were back to his leaving rather than dying.

"Gary Anderson made me a deal," she continued.

"Mom," Rick said softly, calling her *mom* instead of Marissa for the first time I'd heard, "how did you pay Gary Anderson for our vasectomies?"

"In the only currency I had available," she snapped. "I was just trying to do the right thing for my boys. I didn't want you to end up with a bunch of kids to support."

"Like you did?"

"I did what I had to do." She glared at him defiantly.

What a family.

I made myself a mental note to call my mother and invite her and Dad over for dinner then create a special chocolate treat just for them. There are

234

dysfunctional families, and then there are DYSFUNCTIONAL families.

"I hate to break up this family reunion," Fred said, "but I need to see you in private, Rick. This will just take a few minutes."

Like a zombie, Rick moved across the patio and into the house. More entertainment. I followed.

Fred sat down at the small kitchen table and flipped his folder open. I recognized my divorce papers.

"Where did you get those?" I asked.

"From Jason."

"My lawyer? Is Jason a member of...?" I looked at Rick who was still standing, apparently in shock from becoming a new father. "You know, the Donato people."

"Of course not. Please sit down, Rick. We need to go over some details before you sign these documents."

Rick blinked a couple of times then looked at the papers. He sank into a chair but shook his head. "No, I'm not signing. I've had a lot of time to think, and I realize how important you are to me, Lindsay. Look at my family. You see what I've had to overcome. Anything good I've done with my life has been because of you."

I sat down between the two men and rested my elbows on the table. "I can't think of one single thing you've done good with your life."

"And I have no chance of doing anything if I don't have you in my life. You're the best thing that's ever happened to me. Please don't give up on us."

Fred cleared his throat. "In light of new data, Lindsay's reconsidered her demands for the settlement." *I had?* "If she has to go to court, she's going to ask for exactly what she's entitled to, fifty percent of everything."

Rick laughed and leaned back in his chair. "Considering how much money I invested in those properties for that shopping center that's not going to happen now because nobody's going to want to buy clothes or ice cream on top of a crime scene, she'll be lucky to get what she's already asking for."

Fred quietly slid a couple of sheets of paper from the back of the file. "With the addition of these three bank accounts I found plus the one in the Cayman Islands, the condo on Padre Island and the two season tickets to the Chiefs games, I think Lindsay stands to come out quite well on a fifty/fifty settlement."

Rick shot forward to the edge of the chair, the blood visibly draining from his face. "How did you...?"

I folded my arms and glared at Rick. Suddenly I'd like to take him to court and get half of everything, not because I wanted it but just because I didn't want him to have it. "We know everything," I said. "If you want to keep the shirt on your back...which is pretty dirty, by the way, but I guess that happens when you have a son...you need to sign these papers right now."

Fred whipped out a pen.

Perspiration beaded on Rick's upper lip. He drew a hand over it and shook his head. "Those have to be signed in front of a notary and witnesses."

Fred set a stamp on the table beside the pen. "I'm a notary, and we have a yard full of witnesses. I'm sure they'll all be happy to get Lindsay out of your life just in case you die again and they can get their hands on your estate without having to share with her."

Fred was right. Rick did make me a happy woman. I walked out that door clutching that folder with the signed papers, smiling a bigger smile than I could remember.

However, after I called Trent and told him the news, I expected him to put an even bigger smile on my face before the night was over.

THE END

Read on for some of Lindsay's favorite recipes.

Cookie Dough Cheesecake Bars

Cookie Dough:
3 Tbsp. butter, softened
1/2 c. brown sugar
1/2 egg (approximately 2 Tbsp.)
1/8 tsp. baking soda
Dash of salt
3/4 c. flour
1 tsp. vanilla
1/2 c. (rounded or heaped) miniature chocolate chips

Cream together butter and sugar. Stir in egg. Mix flour, salt and baking soda and add to mixture. Add vanilla. Stir in chocolate chips.

Put mixture into refrigerator while mixing cheesecake.

Cheesecake:
4 (8-oz) packages cream cheese, softened
1-1/2 c. sugar
1/4 c. flour
Dash of salt
4-1/2 large eggs
2 c. sour cream
1/4 c. cream
2 teaspoon vanilla

Line the bottom of 2 loaf pans or one standard spring-form pan with parchment paper.

Beat cream cheese until smooth. Add sugar and continue beating until well mixed. Add flour and salt and mix well. Add eggs, one at a time, beating continuously. Add sour cream and mix well. Add cream and vanilla and beat until smooth.

Pour approximately half inch of batter into each pan. Dot with pieces of cookie dough. Add another half inch to cover, then dot with pieces of cookie dough again. Add remaining batter to each pan.

Bake 350 degrees for 60 minutes. Turn off oven and open door slightly, leaving cheesecake in the oven for another hour.

Remove and cool half an hour, then remove from pans. Store covered in refrigerator for at least 8 hours to allow cheesecake to ripen.

Slice and serve. Drizzle with Chocolate Ganache or serve plain.

Chocolate Ganache:

9 ounces bittersweet chocolate, chopped
1 c. cream

Heat cream in sauce pan until it steams but doesn't boil. Add chocolate and stir until it dissolves. Remove from heat and cool.

Chocolate Gravy

2 c. sugar
3 or 4 Tbsp. cocoa powder
3 Tbsp. flour
3/4 milk
1 Tbsp. butter
1 tsp. vanilla

Mix sugar, cocoa and flour in saucepan until there are no chocolate lumps. Stir in milk. Cook over medium heat, stirring constantly, until mixture thickens to the consistency of gravy. Add butter and vanilla. Serve over hot, buttered biscuits.

I will not include a recipe here for biscuits. That's Paula's forte, not mine. When left to my own devices, I use Pillsbury Grand frozen biscuits. I'm especially partial to the buttermilk and the southern style. Don't tell Paula.

No-Crust Chocolate Meringue Pie
(naturally gluten-free)

Meringue Shells:
4 egg whites, room temperature
1/4 teaspoon cream of tartar
2 teaspoon vanilla
1 c. sugar

Preheat oven to 275 degrees. Line 2 baking sheets with ungreased parchment paper.

Beat egg whites on low speed until foamy. Add cream of tartar and vanilla. Continue beating until whites begin to hold their shape. Increase speed to medium high and gradually add sugar. Beat until whites form stiff peaks.

Plop onto parchment paper in dollops of about 1/3 cup, roughly the size of a tennis ball cut in half, at least an inch apart. Spread with back of spoon to make a shell, indenting in the middle and building up the sides.

Bake for 1 hour. Turn off oven, leaving shells in the oven with the door closed for an additional 1-1/2 hours. Remove baking sheets to wire racks. Let meringues stand 15 minutes then carefully loosen with a spatula and transfer to wire racks. Let cool completely.

Fill with chocolate meringue filling, Nutella or chocolate mousse. You can even fill with non-chocolate things…but why would you want to?

Chocolate Filling:
(with thanks to Ruth Waller Jones, my cousin)

1-1/2 c. sugar
1/3 c. cornstarch
2 Tbsp. butter
2 squares (2 oz.) unsweetened chocolate, melted
1/4 tsp. salt
3 c. milk (whole or half and half)
4 egg yolks
2 tsp. vanilla

In saucepan blend sugar, cornstarch and salt. Stir milk into beaten egg yolks. Stir milk/egg mixture into dry ingredients. Cook over medium heat, stirring constantly. When mixture begins to steam, add chocolate and butter. Cook until mixture thickens. Add vanilla. Cool, stirring intermittently to keep it smooth.

Chocolate Lemon Pie

Prepare pie crust. Prick all over with fork to prevent air pockets from forming. If you're really OCD, place another pie pan on top of crust. Bake at 400 degrees until edges brown, approximate 10-12 minutes. Allow to cool while preparing filling.

Filling:
1-1/3 c. sugar
Dash of salt
1/3 c. cornstarch
1-3/4 c. water
5 egg yolks
1/2 c. lemon juice
2 Tbsp. melted butter
1 Tbsp. lemon zest
2 tsp. vanilla

Mix together lemon juice and egg yolks. Set aside.

Combine sugar, salt and cornstarch in saucepan, stirring until well mixed. Add water and cook over medium heat, stirring frequently. When mixture becomes clear and thick, slowly add egg yolk and lemon juice mixture, pouring a small stream and stirring constantly. Cook until mixture boils and becomes thick. Remove from heat. Stir in lemon zest, butter and vanilla. Cool slightly and pour into crust. Cool completely.

Chocolate Topping:
9 ounces bittersweet chocolate, chopped
1 c. heavy cream
1/4 c. corn syrup

Place chocolate in glass or metal bowl. Heat corn syrup and cream to point of steam but not boiling. Pour hot mixture over chocolate. Let stand without stirring until chocolate begins to melt. Stir until mixture is smooth. Cool, stirring occasionally, until mixture is thick.

Pour chocolate mixture over cooled pie and spread to completely cover the top of the pie. Refrigerate until ready to serve.

Chocolate Chip Pancakes

2 eggs
1-1/4 c. milk
3 Tbsp. butter, melted
1-1/2 c. flour
1/2 tsp. salt
2 tsp. baking powder
3 Tbsp. sugar
1 c. mini chocolate chips

Mix flour, salt and baking powder and set aside. Beat eggs and milk until well-mixed and foamy. Stir in melted butter. Add dry ingredients and mix until just blended. It will be lumpy. Do not over-mix. Fold in chocolate chips. Drop onto heated griddle. Cook until bubbles start to form. Flip and cook another minute, until lightly brown.

Serve with butter and chocolate syrup or maple syrup.

No Worries Pie Crust

(This pie crust does not contain chocolate. It is merely the device that allows one to lift chocolate pie from the pan. Therefore, I see no point in wasting time on all that cutting the grease in until it's the size of mutated peas. This crust is quick and easy and always flaky...and allows you to spend more time with your chocolate.)

1-1/3 c. flour
1/2 tsp. salt
1/3 c. oil
3 Tbsp. cold milk

Mix flour and salt. Add oil and milk. Mix.

Put between two sheets of wax paper. Roll out to something vaguely resembling a circle.

Remove top layer of paper, then lay it gently back on crust. Flip crust over, remove new top layer (old bottom layer) and discard. Lay pie tin upside down on crust. Flip crust and pan right side up. Remove and discard remaining layer of wax paper.

Flute edges of pie crust by pinching between thumb and forefinger of one hand while pressing finger of other hand between said thumb and forefinger. (Use first knuckles if you have long fingernails.) Some people think this fluting makes it pretty. The truth is, it assures that none of the filling will spill out in case of overfill.

About the Author:

I grew up in a small rural town in southeastern Oklahoma where our favorite entertainment on summer evenings was to sit outside under the stars and tell stories. When I went to bed at night, instead of a lullaby, I got a story. That could be due to the fact that everybody in my family has a singing voice like a bullfrog with laryngitis, but they sure could tell stories—ghost stories, funny stories, happy stories, scary stories.

For as long as I can remember I've been a storyteller. Thank goodness for computers so I can write down my stories. It's hard to make listeners sit still for the length of a book! Like my family's tales, my stories are funny, scary, dramatic, romantic, paranormal, magic.

Besides writing, my interests are reading, eating chocolate and riding my Harley.

Contact information is available on my website. I love to talk to readers! And writers. And riders. And computer programmers. And poets and pirates and paupers and pawns and kings and cats and dogs. Okay, I just plain love to talk!

http://www.sallyberneathy.com

Made in the USA
Columbia, SC
27 March 2023

14376994R00137